A Kiss
from Cupid

you're my must,
my love!

A Kiss from Cupid

CARLY HUSS

Black Lyon Publishing, LLC

A KISS FROM CUPID

Our books may be ordered through your local bookstore or by visiting the publisher:

www.BlackLyonPublishing.com

Black Lyon Publishing, LLC
PO Box 567
Baker City, OR 97814

This is a work of fiction. All of the charactèrs, names, events, organizations and conversations in this novel are either the products of the author's vivid imagination or are used in a fictitious way for the purposes of this story.

Cover Illustration: Kailyn McQuisten

ISBN-13: 978-1-934912-90-4
Library of Congress Control Number: 2020933019

Published and printed in the United States of America.

Black Lyon
Paranormal RomCom

For the girls who wonder when it
will be their turn to find true love.

Chapter One

$\mathscr{M}$y heartbeat sped to match the rhythm of my wings when I recognized the signs—nervous giggles, lowered lashes, waiting glances. I was about to watch Destiny happen.

I made a sofa out of a mulberry tree that hung low over the porch. Pulling tissues and my stash of Milk Duds from my clutch, I settled in to watch the most romantic moment of my assignment's relationship.

Fiddling with her keys, Jenny blinked her big, doe eyes at Ivan who stared at her waiting lips. He took a step closer, sliding a trembling hand around her waist.

I clasped my hands, anticipating the moment when their lips would touch. Her pink sparks would mingle with his blue ones; they'd blend together, bonding their love irrevocably.

My insides turned all gooey.

Just when I didn't think I could stand waiting for another second, he finally leaned down as she tilted up. Here it was—the moment I'd been waiting for all night.

But it didn't happen.

Before Ivan's lips landed on Jenny's, he blinked as if coming out of a fog. She was still leaning—eyes closed and on the very tips of her toes—but instead of his lips catching hers, he backed away. Her eyes opened, first to slits, then wider as she realized the kiss wasn't going to happen.

"I'm sorry," Ivan said, shaking his head. "I can't."

Her eyes, which had been so happy, turned misty. She didn't say anything as he turned and walked away, leaving her alone on the porch.

Milk Duds fell from my lap as I zoomed off my tree, ready

to go to her. And do what? I didn't know. But I couldn't sit by and watch her heart break into a thousand, million, trillion, tiny pieces. He was it. Her Fated. The man made especially for her. And he'd just left her.

I was inches above Jenny, trying to decide what to say to her when someone grabbed the base of my wings.

I didn't need eyes in the back of my head to know the Paver who'd stopped me was Rupert. His cologne gave him away. A thick, timber smell that made my lady parts feel all sorts of good, but made the rest of me crazy, and not in the fun way.

"Put me down," I shrieked, bending and jerking. My wings fluttered behind me, but no matter how hard I tried, I couldn't break free of his hold.

"Not until you promise to behave yourself," Rupert said.

I blew fury through my clenched teeth as I swatted behind me. If I could land just one of my nails on his perfect little face, I'd be a happy Cupid.

Unaware of the chaos above her, the heartbroken girl slipped into her house to mourn the loss of her love behind her closed door.

I was still struggling against Rupert when he un-pinched my wings. My momentum sent me flying toward the ground. Too late to do anything about the fact that I was about to eat concrete, I slammed my eyes together and tried my best to protect my face with my arms.

I never hit the ground. Rupert's big arms scooped me out of the air, holding me like an over-sized baby. I crossed my arms and pointed my chin away as he flew us to the mulberry tree.

"Now, do you promise to be a good little Freya?" he asked, depositing me on a branch.

"You're lucky I'm a lady, or I'd spit on you."

Rupert lifted a brow. "I don't think a true lady would talk about spit."

He was right, and that made me want to do it even more.

"What are you doing here?" I asked, smoothing out my skirts and plucking fallen tissues from leaves.

"Same as you." Rupert winked, and I hated that he looked good doing it. "Stalking random, unsuspecting couples." The branch dipped when he landed next to me. He leaned back and propped his feet on my leg.

"I am not stalking them." I shoved his loafers off my dress and lifted myself from the branch, hovering in front of him. "And they aren't random. They're my assignment."

Rupert's enormous chest shook with laughter. "Tell yourself what you want, but watching someone when they don't know you're there is textbook stalking."

I shot him my best haughty look. "Then I guess that means you were stalking me."

"Not true. I let you know as soon as I got here. And it's a good thing I showed up and saved you from yourself."

"I didn't need your saving."

"Your Veil was half down. You would have exposed yourself in front of that girl if I hadn't stopped you."

I huffed and rolled my eyes, but he was right. If I'd let my Veil fall in my desperation to comfort her, there would have been no way to explain the five-foot-five Cupid flying above her. At the very least, I'd have a lot of paperwork to do. But more likely, I'd get my Veil revoked.

"What were you doing?" Rupert asked. Leaves rustled when he sprung from the branch. "Why were you going to risk being seen?" He flew so close to me our wings touched.

The sensation of his silky wings caressing mine made me feel heady. Or maybe that was his cologne. Either way, I backed up. "They didn't Seal the Kiss."

He scoffed. "Impossible."

"I know it's supposed to be impossible, but obviously it isn't. They were so close. All the signs were there—pink cheeks, giggles, eye contact. But then, he didn't kiss her."

"You must have messed something up. You sure you kissed both of them?"

I hoped the glare I shot his way told him how moronic I thought he was. "You don't forget kissing someone." What was I saying? This was Rupert I was talking to. "Well, you might forget kissing someone, but I don't."

The material of his shirt stretched over his broad shoulders when he crossed his arms. "Then how do you explain it?"

I riffled through my memories from my training. It was such a simple process: Kiss Fated A, Kiss Fated B, wait for them to Seal the Kiss.

"Did you kiss both of them within twenty-four hours?" he asked.

"Yes. And before you ask, they met within the next twenty-four."

He shrugged. "Free will. It's the bane of our existence, baby."

"I told you not to call me that," I said, diving into a gust of wind, not caring where it took me as long as it was far away from him. His chuckle followed me, but blessedly he didn't.

♥

I wound up on the south side of The Paver's Cloud, above the bright city lights of Downtown Dallas. It didn't matter how many times I'd seen the glowing ball of the Reunion Tower, or the purple lights of the Omni Hotel, I still took the time to appreciate the beauty of the Dallas skyline. The sheer size of the buildings and the miles of lights were a constant reminder of all the potential love the city held.

I longed to hover above the streets to scope out budding romances and do a little off-the-clock Cupiding, but Rupert's taunts echoed in my mind. I soared higher, heading straight for the back entrance of the Paver's Cloud above the city.

The Veil that hid The Paver's Cloud from planes and star-gazers was as invisible to me as it was to humans until I broke the barrier. Only then, could I see the floating city. The Paver's Cloud wasn't filled with skyscrapers or neon lights, but it held a beauty of its own. If a fairy tale and space opera had a love child, the result would have been the series clouds cradling diamond-shaped office buildings, stacked shops, and rows of multi-colored apartments.

As soon as I passed through the Veil, my skin tightened. Getting high on other peoples' love lives wasn't the only reason I wanted to stay among the crowds in the lower city. If I lived down there with them, instead of a mini-city in the sky, I could choose where I had my after-work drink. Or maybe I'd go out dancing or watch a movie in a theater. But no, I headed over to The Parched Paver to meet up with the same group of people, order the same drink from the same bartender, and dodge the same lame pick-up lines from the same barflies. Don't get me wrong, I loved my people, and I enjoyed my routine, but I wished I had choices.

I sailed straight past the business airway and into the city's center, and flew up three stories and into The Parched Paver's front door. I flitted my way above seated Pavers. Like usual, Lana beat me there and had already ordered our drinks.

The bartender placed a tall, pink cocktail in front of me. "Cosmo for you," Dave said. "And a house brew for Lana." His stare lingered on my friend as he handed her a mug of foamy, amber liquid.

"Thanks, Dave," I said, kicking Lana's leg under the table with my cherry pump.

"Ow. Chill out." Lana said in her smooth, lazy voice. "What was that for?"

"Your obliviousness." I looked meaningfully to Dave and raised an eyebrow. "He's in love with you."

"You think everyone's in love with everyone. Aren't you sick of playing matchmaker?" Lana asked, though, I caught her peering over her beer to sneak a peek at Dave.

"Never." I smiled, but the grin stopped before reaching its full potential when I remembered the look on Jenny's face. How could Ivan have not Sealed the Kiss?

"Painting is my one and only love," Lana said. "I spent the entire day watching my assignment paint the most beautiful sunrise. It inspired me."

"I see that." I pointed to a sky-blue spot on her chin. "Painting the flavor of the week, is it?"

"No. Painting is the new love of my life." She choked on a swig of her beer and nodded to the doorway. "Speaking of, here comes the love of your life."

I followed her gaze, hoping to see a barrel-chested Scotsman on a horse with a bouquet of heather.

It was just Rupert and his cologne. Had he flown home and sprayed more on since I saw him last, or did he keep a bottle in his pocket?

I averted my eyes to make the message clear—he was not welcome.

It didn't work. His hand slid over my shoulders as he pulled a chair from an adjacent table.

"Ugh. What do you want? Haven't you harassed me enough today?"

He leaned in, his mouth dangerously close to my ear. "I think you know what I want."

His words sent a crawling sensation over my neck as if he'd planted a bug via his breath. I shifted my shoulders to shrug him off and swatted the imaginary insect. He dropped his arm from around my shoulder, but he didn't leave me alone. He stood behind me, and I felt his fingers on the bow that secured my dress at the base of my neck.

"What are you doing?" With my eyes, I begged Lana to intervene, but she was too busy staring at her masterpiece to pay attention.

"Looking for the tag. I want to find out where you were made. From the looks of you, I'd say you were made in heaven."

"Oh, buzz off!" I slapped his hand and turned so he could see the fury in my eyes.

Lana finally pulled her eyes away from her canvas and said, "Isn't there someone more desperate waiting for you to use one of your bad lines on?" She used her beer to point at the women ogling Rupert.

"Not any I haven't Sealed the deal with." Rupert flashed his most unappealing, yet somehow charming grin.

"Your bad lines actually work?" I asked.

"On everyone but you, baby." He slung his arm back around my shoulders. His chocolate eyes stared into my green ones, his eyebrows pulling together in dramatic confusion.

I shrank away from him. "What?"

"You have something …" He used his index finger to point at my right eye.

I blinked several times but didn't feel anything. "What is it?"

"Just a sparkle. My mistake."

"Ugh, go away." I hid a laugh by emptying the rest of my Cosmo into my mouth.

"Just one time, baby. I promise you won't regret it."

I slammed my empty glass on the table. "You think

promising me a one-night stand is gonna work? I don't get you. We're Cupids."

"Now you've done it," Lana said, knowing I was about to get on my soapbox.

"The whole point of our existence," I continued, "is to create epic love and life-long romances filled with meaningful, true passion."

Rupert and Lana said the last few words with me.

"And you think the promise of some meaningless night will hold any interest for me whatsoever?"

"That's why we should take advantage of our freedom while we have it. Someday a Cupid's gonna show up and perform their Kiss of Death on us, and we'll be strapped down to one person for the rest of our lives. We should take as many test drives as possible before we buy a car."

"You're disgusting," I said.

"You're afraid if you let yourself be with me, you'll never want anyone else."

"That's exactly right. I'm afraid that after one night with you, I'll never be satisfied again."

"At least you're admitting it." Rupert looked at me for another moment then exhaled in defeat. "How about a kiss?"

"The only way you'll ever receive a kiss from me is if I'm the Cupid assigned to the poor, unfortunate soul who's stuck with you for the rest of her life."

"And thus with a kiss, I die," he quoted, bringing his hand to his heart and pretending to faint.

Dave made his way back to our table with another Cosmo for me and an Old Fashioned for Rupert. "Okay, Rupe. You've had your fun tonight. Leave Freya alone. You know if she gets her petticoat in a twist, you're gonna get a slap in the face." The tilting corners of Dave's mouth seemed to say that he wouldn't be too unhappy if Rupert ignored his warning, and I ended up slapping him after all.

I beamed at Dave, holding my new cocktail to him with a nod.

Rupert ignored Dave and made himself comfortable. "What are you ladies up to tonight?"

"I'm getting back to my art, that's what." Lana threw cash

down and shoved her wallet into her hand-made purse. "I'll see you down there tomorrow, Frey." The beads at the end of her long dreadlocks jangled all the way out of the pub.

I slumped. I hadn't even gotten the chance to tell Lana about the failed Kiss. Since she was a Muse, she wouldn't have any unknown Cupid insight for me, but Lana had a way of saying the exact right thing to make me feel better. And stupid Rupert had scared her off.

"I can still hear her," Rupert pointed out after Lana was out of sight.

"No kidding."

My laugh faded away, and a cloud of awkwardness hovered over our table. Neither of us knew what to say now that his bag of pick-up lines had been depleted. I swirled my drink around in its pretty glass. He took a sip from his Old Fashioned and caught an ice cube in his brilliant, white teeth. I couldn't help but notice that if his mouth were used as anything other than a vehicle for inappropriate comments, it had the potential to create a nice smile.

If pressed, I'd admit he was quite handsome. He was no Scotsman on horseback, but he was tall with an athletic build and broad shoulders. His dark hair was always styled flawlessly. It hung over his forehead, attracting attention to his deep, brown eyes. Tall, dark, and handsome. He could be a model. He practically modeled for Ralph Lauren already since all he wore was their Polo shirts.

I found myself appreciating his good looks and wishing I could break through his Fate's-gift-to-women-façade when he opened his mouth, reminding me why he made my skin crawl.

"I'm giving you one last chance to test drive this ride before I cruise over to Jacqueline and make her dreams come true."

"Hard pass."

"Your loss," he said, strutting to the table where Jacqueline and Natasha giggled.

I never understood how they came into their classifications. As an Elve, Jacqueline was meant to maintain the balance of lives in the world—acting as a guardian angel and Grimm Reaper at the same time. And Natasha's classification as an Oracle was possibly the most crucial of all Pavers. Her job was to whisper each person's Destiny into their ear when they were born, so even as wailing, tiny balls of toes and tummies, they begin to strive to fulfill their Destiny. The two bimbos had been given more responsibility than I thought they deserved.

"Hi, handsome," Jacqueline said, wiggling her finger into Rupert's belt loop.

I sipped my Cosmo, trying to wash away the taste of envy. I had no reason to feel bitter. Rupert had come to me first, and I'd declined his offer. I couldn't peel my eyes away from them though. Rupert shot me a wink, and Jacqueline glared.

"Uh oh," a soprano voice said from behind me.

"Someone has a frenemy," a twin voice, just as high-pitched but with a male tone added.

I turned to find Percy and Penny sitting in the previously empty chairs. Percy lounged with his feet on the table, and Penny sat cross-legged in her chair. They passed their ever-moving bouncy ball back and forth between them.

"You know he's in love with you, right?" Percy asked before releasing the ball in Penny's direction.

"Absolutely in love with you." Penny caught the ball.

"What? No he's not." Heat burned my cheeks. "He doesn't love me. He doesn't even know what love is. He doesn't want to know what it is."

"That's what you think," Penny sang.

"Not what we think," Percy harmonized.

"Well, y'all need to think differently, because you're wrong. The only thing he loves is himself." I twitched my lips. "And possibly his cologne."

The twins exchanged meaningful looks.

"What was that?" I gestured between them.

"What was what?" they asked together.

"That look you two shared. What does that mean?" I reached out and snagged the ball out of the air. "What do you know?"

Four wide, blue eyes stared at me. Their faces were similar — round and innocent-looking, only differing in that Penny's lashes were longer, and her eyebrows were tweezed into thin lines.

"We don't know anything." Percy made a pointless grab at

the ball in my hand.

"We only know what we see." Penny pulled a second ball from her purse and tossed it at Percy, who caught it without taking his eyes off me.

"And what do you see?" I tossed the ball back to Percy. There wasn't a point of holding onto it if they had another one. Percy refrained from throwing the balls back at Penny. Instead, he kept them both in his hands, rotating them around themselves. "Every day he waits until you show up before he makes his move on anyone else."

"You're always his first choice," Penny added.

"Of course I'm his first choice. I'm the only one he hasn't conquered. I'm a constant reminder that he is resistible."

Penny cocked her head to the side. "He hasn't conquered me."

"Or me." Percy laughed.

Penny snatched the balls from Percy. "And he hasn't taken Lana home."

That was true. He'd never made so much as a pass at Lana. "She would never go for a pretty boy like Rupert."

"So you admit he's pretty?" Percy joked.

Penny shot the ball at Percy's head.

He caught it in his mouth. "What's gotten into you?" he mumbled around the pink ball.

"Nothing's gotten into me. I just think it's sweet how Rupert obviously loves Freya so much, and she doesn't even see it."

"Okay, I've had enough of this crazy-talk," I said, standing and smoothing my hands over the length of my dress's skirt. I threw down enough cash to cover my drink and a big tip. "I'm going home."

"Leaving already?" Rupert's teasing voice said from behind me.

I stumbled over my feet as I turned toward him. "Finished already?" I quipped.

"I realized I forgot something."

"What?"

"You."

I groaned. "You're exhausting."

"Just kidding." He winked. "I forgot to pay Dave." Rupert

opened his wallet and shuffled through a wad of bills. "Plus, Jacqueline got all 'so, where is this going?' and I was so not in the mood for that conversation, so I bounced."

"How gentlemanly of you."

"I'm saving all of my gentlemanly-ness for you, Freya." He dipped into a low bow, took my hand, and kissed it. "When are you going to believe me when I say you're my one and only?"

I jerked my hand out of his. "You are so full of … of …"

"Full of what?" His eyes widened. He tried to hide a smile, but a dimple appeared, betraying him.

"Oh, I know what he's full of. Pick me, pick me!" Percy's hand darted in the air, raised above his head like a child waiting to be called upon in class.

Penny's hand soared skyward, trying to be taller than her brother. "No! Pick me!"

Rupert stroked his chin, glancing between the two of them. "I choose …" His finger danced back and forth between the twins but finally landed on my nose. "Freya. I want to hear you say a naughty word." His hand slid lightly between my cardigan's buttons and into the top of my dress, leaving behind a foreign object in my cleavage.

Not soon enough, my reflexes got the chance to slap his hand away. "The only dirty word I'm going to say is what you are."

"And that is?" Rupert's eyebrows raised in anticipation.

Penny and Percy took turns supplying options for me to choose from, "Walking Boner! Bastard! Taco Stuffer! Man Slut! Horn Dog!"

"You're a … a … a pig!"

"Oooh, your words burn me." Rupert chuckled.

The twins deflated with disappointment before they resumed tossing both balls back and forth between them, double time.

"Thanks for letting me buy your drink." With a wink, he turned and walked out of the bar.

I reached into my cleavage, embarrassed by the indecent act, and pulled out cash. It was twice the amount I'd left on the table for my bill. Not wanting to accept his money, I threw it on the table. *That'll make Dave's night.*

"Dom dom da dom, dom dom da dom." Percy and Penny sang the wedding march as I stormed out of The Parched Paver.

Chapter Two

The barista called my name, and I took my frozen caffeine and Lana's Chai whatever to the patio table we sat at when the weather was nice. But even if she'd been a block down the street, I'd be able to find her. Like a regular Picasso, Lana sat behind her easel. I couldn't help but think of how inconvenient it would be to fly around all day with something so huge.

"Is this what you left me alone with Rupert for last night?" I said, plopping into the chair across from her. "I was hoping I'd get to talk to you."

"Well, you have me now," she said, blowing on her drink before taking a sip. "What's up?"

"My assignment last night, they didn't Seal their Kiss."

"The couple you've been working on all week?"

"Yeah. Last night was their last night before the Kiss faded."

"Then Kiss them again. It'll be easier the second time since they already know each other."

"You're right," I said, nodding. "I thought of that too, it just sounds so much easier when you say it."

"That's because the simplest answer is usually the right one, and I look for the easy answer."

"No." I wrinkled my nose. "I think it's because your voice is soothing."

She rolled her eyes but smiled.

"I need another simple answer. But this time I have no ideas."

"Go on."

"Rupert. He's getting out of control. He's always been bad, but the past few days he's been incorrigible. I think he's convinced himself he actually has feelings for me. I know he's convinced the twins. They think he's in love with me."

"Well, he is in love with you," Lana said, a matter of fact.

"Take that back." The truth was, I too was starting to believe that Rupert's feelings for me were genuine. But if I was wrong, and he was just trying extra hard to get in my dress, I didn't think my heart would recover. Not from being used like that. Not by Rupert.

Lana sighed and rested her paintbrush in her cup of water on the table. "I can't take it back. He's in love with you. And he'll remain in love with you as long as you deny him."

My mouth opened to argue, but she raised a finger, indicating for me to listen.

"You want to shake Rupert?"

I nodded, but I could guess that the expression on my face was answer enough.

"Pretend to be in love with him. You said it yourself, he's all freaked out about commitment and blew off Jacqueline just because she wanted to know where they stood. So, throw yourself at him. Talk about getting married and having babies and all that. He'll freak out, and you'll never have to put up with him again."

"Ha. That might work." I curled my lip. "So long as I can stomach playing the part."

"Good. Your crisis has been dealt with. Now, can we focus on me for a second?"

"Oh." I sat straighter. I'd wanted to tell Lana the details of my botched Kiss from last night, but in the twenty-three years I'd known Lana, she never talked about herself. If she had something to say, I'd put my own drama aside and listen to her. "What's going on with you?"

"I need you to tell me what you think of my painting. And be honest. Don't sugarcoat it or wrap it in a pretty bow like you do. Tell me straight. Do you think it's any good?" Lana repositioned her easel, allowing me to see it.

I tilted my head, trying to decipher what I was looking at. I took a long sip from my coffee to buy time. "You decided not to go with the sunset on the ocean, after all?"

Lana clicked her tongue against the gap in her teeth. "It is a sunset on an ocean. Ocean. Sky." She pointed to each half, respectively. "The colors of the sunset reflect off the water, making it have that color. Do you see it now?"

I didn't. "But what about these?" I pointed to what I'd thought were tree trunks.

"Fish."

"And that one?" I pointed to a grey object I'd previously assumed was a leafless tree.

"A dolphin."

"Oh."

"You hate it." It wasn't a question.

"It's not that bad."

Lana took another look at the painting and laughed. "Yes, it is." Her laughs turned cold until I heard a sniffle. "I just want to be good at something. How am I supposed to inspire people to create greatness if I can't create it myself?"

"It doesn't matter if you paint or not. You're a wonderful Muse. Every one of your assignments excels at their talents because you do such a good job of inspiring them."

She rolled her eyes. "All I do is find them and tell their subconscious what to do."

"That's not all you do. Just like I don't find my couple, Kiss them, and be on my merry way. Our jobs take more. You know that."

She shrugged a limp shoulder.

"The assignment card tells you they need to write a song with specific lyrics, but it doesn't tell you the tune. You have to create it in your mind then send it into theirs."

She looked at me with hope, so I barreled on, stroking her ego like I knew she needed.

"Or, like when the card says to make your assignment fall in love with film so they'll become an actor, it doesn't say what movie to show them to kick start their fascination. That's all your doing." I pointed at her. "You're the one who brings life to dreams and plants them in people's minds, so they become great. You create the whole vision in your mind. That's a talent in and of itself. I'd never be able to do what you do."

"Really?"

"Really." Wanting to change the subject, I asked, "What's

your assignment today?"

She pulled her assignment card from her cloth purse. She nodded to me, and I fished my own assignment card out of my polka-dot clutch.

My card looked like an award envelope—stiff, red paper, folded into thirds, sealed with a silver heart. Lana's was the same, except hers was gold and sealed with the Celtic symbol for creativity—three swirls connected by a central triangle.

"Bonnie Lopez," Lana said, then paraphrased the details on the cards. "She works at a coffeehouse in Highland Village— barista by day, doodler by night. She sketches all the time but has never done anything with her work. She's destined to be a tattoo artist."

"That sounds fun. You'll get to study her in a big, comfy chair all day, drinking coffee, and making goo-goo eyes at all of your fellow hippies."

"Those are hipsters, not hippies. But you're right. I could have worse assignments. You anywhere close to me?" Lana tried to steal a peek at my card.

I slid my card open with blue fingernails. A picture of a man with leathery, laugh-lined skin and salt-and-pepper hair smiled at me. The card told me his name is Glen Nichols, sixty-eight years old, and retired two years ago from the oil industry. Behind his card, was his Fated. Her sharp, blue eyes pierced through her soft, wrinkled skin. Anna Novakova, seventy-one, and teaches history to middle-schoolers.

"Old people?" Lana asked over my shoulder.

"Yeah." I shrugged with a smile. "I like Fating old people. They usually aren't expecting to find another great love of their life, so they're more appreciative."

"I guess—but it doesn't seem fair that they get to have two Fateds when most of us are still waiting around for our first."

I couldn't argue with her there. As Pavers, Lana and I both appeared to be teenagers, and in most ways, we still were, but we technically were in our twenties and ready for the love of our lives to come knocking. Me especially.

"I didn't think you cared about your Fated, Miss My Art is the One and Only Love of My Life."

Pink filled in the gaps between Lana's freckles. "I don't. I was talking about you."

"Sure, you were."

"Cut it out. Where are they? Close to me?"

I shook my head. "Irving."

She frowned. We wouldn't be able to meet for lunch.

"How are you going to get them to meet? I doubt they get to the clubs often," Lana joked.

"You have your talents, and I have mine."

♥

I rode the wind as I made my way to my first stop, thinking back on the advice I'd given Lana. When I'd told her that our jobs were more than just planting the creative seed and kissing our Fated, I had been talking for her benefit. And in her case, it really was true. She had to craft a whole scene to inspire her assignments. Her job wouldn't work if she just showed up and touched them.

But me? I liked to create a mood, make sure they met under the perfect circumstances, add music for flourish, but none of that was a requirement. If two Fateds met in front of a dumpster or at the beach at sunset, it wouldn't change anything. Once they'd received Cupid's Kiss, they'd find each other no matter what and Seal the Kiss.

Or so I thought until yesterday.

If a Cupid's job was to Kiss one Fated and then the other, and Destiny did the rest, then why were we told to make sure the Kiss had been Sealed? Most Cupids, like Rupert, Kissed them and checked back the required week later to make sure all went as planned. I was one of the few who enjoyed watching the Sealing, but either way, we all had to see the purple sparks at one point or another. Why would it be necessary if it wasn't as guaranteed as we were told?

Something had gone wrong with my Fated, and that couldn't have been the first time in the history of Destiny that it had happened, or we wouldn't be required to check back. Could Rupert have figured it out so easily? Could it have been due to free will?

That was the whole point of Pavers anyways, to put Destiny

back on course when free will got in the way. But supposedly, Fateds were so perfect for each other that they would have chosen each other if they found one another on their own. Cupids just helped speed the process if their lives had derailed them from finding each other by the time they were supposed to.

As I got close to my first stop, I let myself fall slowly so I could clear my mind of questions. If I had anything to do with the failed Sealing, I wouldn't let it happen again.

Chapter Three

$\mathcal{G}$lenn's house was not what I'd expected. When I'd read "oil industry" on his Fated card, I pictured millionaire, but his modest, home in the not-so-great side of town painted a picture of a different life in my mind. He hadn't been counting his money while waiting for the next deposit into his bank account, he'd been working in the field with heavy machinery and back-breaking labor.

But working with his hands must have been what made him happy, because I found him in his yard, tending to his plants.

A soft hum filled my ears when I got close enough, and I realized the sound was coming from Glen. He couldn't hear me in my Veil, but I was as silent as possible when I flew closer so I could make out what he was saying.

He wasn't saying anything. He was singing. Hobbling from one tomato plant to the next, he pruned away dead leaves and checked for ripeness. The song was one I'd recognized from old movies I always associated with falling in love. How perfect that I caught him singing a love song when today would be the day he would find his love.

I imagined a second voice singing along with him as he and Anna gardened away the last quarter of their lives.

I was careful to land in the grass so I wouldn't trample over seedlings or tiny sprouts in the rows of soil. He plopped five perfectly red tomatoes in his bag before turning away from the garden. He faced me head on, walking without hurry, proudly carrying his lute. I waited until he was only a foot away before I leaned in and lightly pressed my lips to his.

Blue dust, only I could see, sparked from his lips and floated into the sky to begin their journey of searching for their mate.

♥

Anna wasn't as easy to find. The GPS on my phone took me to her school with ease but locating her within the building wasn't as simple as following a map.

Mrs. Novakova's door was open wide as the kids funneled in. Boys with gelled hair and too many pimples avoided the girls with blue eyeshadow who smiled longingly at them with braces-covered teeth.

As I shuffled in with them, memories of the most awkward years of my life poured into me. In The Paver's Cloud, middle school was when we were finally separated into classifications so we could learn how to be the best Pavers we could be. Cupids had it the worst because we knew we'd have to practice our Kisses on each other, putting the worst kind of pressure on kids going through puberty.

I shook off memories of breath mints and nervous sweats to focus on Anna.

She was standing in the front of the class talking to a student about the homework assignment that was due. From what I understood, he'd left it in the car that morning. Mrs. Novakova seemed to feel pity for the kid as she frowned. "If I make an exception for you, I'll have to make exceptions for everyone. The assignment was due at the beginning of the period. I'm sorry, but you can turn in the paper tomorrow, but it will be late."

"Yes, Mrs. Novakova." The boy looked to the floor as he walked to his desk.

Before I had the chance to perform Cupid's Kiss, the last student to enter the room closed the door behind her. The sound was the last thing an invisible Paver wanted to hear. A phantom door opening would be noticed in a room with thirty bored middle-schoolers. It seemed I would be receiving a history lesson.

I settled on the ground between two rows of desks to give my wings a rest when Anna told the students to turn to page 462.

"Today's topic is especially close to my heart—Modern Immigration," Anna said with a slight accent, European if I had to guess. "The last few weeks we learned about American colonization in the seventeenth and eighteen centuries, but even after the cities were built and states were made, people from all around the world continued to immigrate to the US to live out the American Dream."

The lesson was as much about Modern Immigration as it was about Anna Novakova. She seamlessly combined her personal experience as a young Czechoslovakian immigrant with the history of the rest of the twentieth-century immigrants.

"So did it work?" A girl in the back of the class asked, without waiting for her name to be called.

"Did what work?"

"The American Dream. You said your mom and dad moved here to escape the communist rule and to live out the American dream. So did it work? Are you living it?"

Anna's smile was thin as she nodded. "Yes and no." Her laugh was hollow. "The American Dream means something different to everyone. My father wanted to bring his family to a safe home where he worked for fair pay and provide for my mother, my brother, and me, so we could grow up and do the same for our families. My father got a good job, and we lived comfortably, so yes. But my brother's wife cannot have children, and I'm still waiting for my prince charming, so I am very sad to say that we failed my father in the second half of his dream."

If I had been flying, my wings would have stopped. Anna Novakova was seventy-one years old, and she was still waiting to fall in love. That meant Glen Nichols wasn't the man she was fated to spend the last chapter of her life with, he was the man she fated to for her whole life, and she wasn't destined to meet him until her life was almost over.

I rose to my feet and walked to Anna with purpose—more eager to give her Cupid's Kiss than I'd ever been before. I couldn't wait for her to spend lazy mornings with Glen in his garden, singing songs from old movies, and dancing among the tomatoes at sunset.

I barely had the patience to wait for her to finish her sentence before I planted the Kiss on her. The pink dust sparked off her lips, and I knew it would find Glen's in the sky. And as they merged, Destiny would take over, and they'd be pulled to each other like magnets.

I spent the rest of the class period trying to imagine how this woman could have lived seventy-one years without finding her Fated. Every day, matches in their teens met on their own, not needing Cupid's Kiss to find the person Destiny intended them to be with. Anna had to wait to the end of her life to find her Fated. It didn't seem fair.

The children were working on an assignment for the last few minutes of class, so I took the opportunity to really study her, as she walked around the room to answer questions, hoping to find a reason she never married or fell in love.

She seemed to be a pleasant woman. She was patient and kind to her students as they asked questions. I even noticed she talked to the boy who'd forgotten his homework and told him that if he could get someone to bring his completed assignment to her before the end of the school day, she'd allow him to receive full credit, showing she had a forgiving nature. Even at seventy-one, Anna could still be called beautiful. Sure, her skin sagged and creased, and her hair was more silver than brown, but the shape of her lips and set of her piercing blue eyes were as clear as I was sure they'd been in her twenties.

I hoped I would age as gracefully as she had when my Hundred was over, and I resumed the aging process. I could see myself as clearly as I could see her standing in front of me. My green eyes would shine as brightly, and my lips would still be painted into their red bow-shape, though I didn't think I would have the courage to stop dying my hair like Anna did. But I could see the likenesses in our bone structure and petite, curvy frame.

My blood turned to ice when I imagined more possible similarities. What if, like her, I wasn't destined to meet my Fated until I was seventy-one? Which would really be one-hundred-and-seventy-one.

Pavers lived normal lives, aging at a normal rate, until we graduated from our Classification Schooling, then the aging processes stunted for one hundred years while we served as

Pavers in the field. When our Hundred was over, we'd resume aging right where we left off, and raised our families and worked within The Paver's Cloud as supervisors, store owners, and other necessary jobs. Some Pavers met their Fated during their field years, others met theirs before even graduating, but a small amount wouldn't find their Fated until after they've served their Hundred.

I couldn't imagine being alone for that long. The thought was one of the most depressing I'd ever let myself entertain. It made me understand why Rupert wasn't waiting around for a Cupid's Kiss that may not come for another century.

Another *century*.

I imagined how lonely every night of my long life had the potential to be.

As if I could control my own Destiny by controlling Anna's, I made it my mission to make sure not even one extra minute went by without Glen. The same thing would not happen to them as it did to my couple last night.

I hovered above the door like a bull waiting for a student to finally open the door and let me out of my pen. As soon as the door opened, I was soaring through halls, barely noticing the students spilling out of the classrooms and into the hallways. I couldn't get out of there fast enough.

My phone buzzed in my purse. I slowed my flight just enough so I could open my purse without dropping its contents all over the Metroplex. I'd done that before.

It was a text from Lana. "This one is gonna take a while. Not gonna make it to the PP tonight."

"Same here." I wouldn't sleep again until they met. I would be on them like Rupert on a blonde until they Sealed their Kiss. My part was supposed to be over. Cupid's Kiss was absolute— the moment I'd kissed Anna, finishing the second half of my task, their pink and blue sparks collided, pulling them toward each other. Depending on the couple, it could take them minutes or weeks to Seal the Kiss, creating the unbreakable bond. I couldn't stand knowing Anna had to wait one more minute, let alone weeks.

I was hovering above Glen's house before a plan had formulated. Lana's club joke rang through my mind. She was right. How was I going to get them to meet?

I toyed with the idea of calling them both, pretending to be a friend who wanted to meet them for dinner—it had worked on other couples—but I hadn't spent enough time with them to learn who to impersonate.

Glen came out his front door before I'd formulated a plan. He had changed out of his gardening clothes and into a nice pair of slacks coupled with a button-down shirt despite the heat of the Texas summer sun. He must be going somewhere important. If I figured out where he was going, I could find a way to make Anna go there too.

I followed Glen's car closely as he drove, still trying to come up with a plan. I'd almost settled on lifting the Veil and getting involved directly when I noticed the direction the car was driving. Toward the school.

He obviously wasn't going to the actual school, but if I could somehow fly into the school, convince Anna to come outside before Glen drove past, and he saw her, they'd have to Seal the Kiss.

But then, he turned into the school's parking lot. And then he parked. And then he got out of the car. And walked to the school.

I couldn't believe my eyes as I followed Glen to the front desk where he told the receptionist he was looking for Ms. Novakova.

I watched miracles like this come to be every day, but I was still awestruck by how powerful Cupid's magnetism was. The blue stream of dust flew above him, flying through the air above everyone's head. It was on a mission.

"There she is," the receptionist said, pointing to Anna. She carried herself with the poise of a queen through the school's hallway.

Her pink dust propelled itself forward, pulling her like a tether to its match. The pink and blue streams found each other above the girl's restroom. And as soon as it happened, their heads snapped to each other.

Glen gripped the folder in his hand tighter, walking away from the receptionist. "I see her."

Anna's feet sped up, carrying her more like a young, excited princess than a regal queen.

"Glen," she said, her voice light and surprised.

"Anna," Glen said, shaking his head. "When Bradley told me I had to bring his work to Ms. Novakova, I wondered if it was … but it couldn't have been possible."

She laughed and nodded. "Every time I saw the name Nichols on Bradley's papers, I'd thought, maybe, but it's such a common name that …" She waved away the idea.

"What are the chances?" His hand was on her face, taking in this woman he'd apparently known from long ago.

"How's Claudette?"

He shook his head. "Died nineteen years ago."

She gripped the hand that was on her cheek. "Oh Glen, I'm so sorry to hear that."

"Don't be. She's at peace." His eyes didn't stop searching her face. "Anna Novakova."

Her laugh sounded like bells. "Fifty-four years, and you still can't say it right."

"Fifty-four years, and I'll bet you still like how I say it best."

Her nod was emphatic. "I do."

The pink and blue sparks flew off their lips in a firework, leaving purple dust in its wake.

Kids whooped and cat-called, and I was cheering right along side them, pumping my fists in the air as I hovered above them.

Embarrassed, Anna pulled away from Glen and told the kids to get to their classes, but her heart wasn't in it. She kept Glen's hand close to her heart as she stared back at him. "I waited fifty-four years for this moment."

Chapter Four

"You're calling it 'a day' early," Rupert said, catching up to me as we approached the Veil that masked The Paver's Cloud.

Below us were miles and miles of cars stuck in rush hour traffic. Car fumes wafted to the top of the Dallas skyline. It was the worst time of day to be flying toward the Texas sun.

I wiped a bead of sweat from my brow. "So are you."

"I always get done early. I'm the fastest Cupid in the city. You're the one who likes to swoon over your matches and create the most magical setting possible." Rupert's voice swung this way and that, letting me know how stupid he thought the concept was.

"Yeah, well, not today."

"Hey, easy, what's wrong?" Rupert asked, as genuinely as was possible for him.

"Nothing's wrong. I just don't feel particularly romantic today."

"That's all?"

I considered telling him yes, but then thought better of it. Rupert's outlook on romance and love couldn't have been more different than mine. However, his insight might help me come to terms with a possible lonely Hundred.

"I Kissed a couple in their seventies today."

"So?"

"Do you want me to talk to you or not?"

"Sorry, I'll be on my best behavior." In front of me, Rupert flew backward, crossed one leg over his knee and placed his clasped hands in his lap.

I rolled my eyes. "She'd never been in love before, and it got me thinking. What if I don't get my Cupid's Kiss until after I finish with my Hundred?"

Rupert straightened. "Freya, come on. You don't really think that's possible, do you?"

"Why not? It doesn't happen a lot, sure, but it does happen. Marisol has been done with her Oracle service for years, and a Cupid hasn't come to her yet."

"What I mean, is it isn't possible that you won't fall in love before that. No one says you have to receive the Kiss to find your Fated. More often than not, we Pavers find our Fated on our own since we all live so close together. You've probably already met yours."

"But what if I am the small percentage of people who have to wait for a Cupid, but the Cupid doesn't come until I'm old. I can't wait that long, I'm already tired of waiting."

"You're not listening to what I'm saying." Rupert stopped flying and grabbed my shoulders to secure my attention. "There's no way that you, Freya Darling, will go one hundred years without finding someone to love you. You're too good, too nice, too beautiful for guys to pass up. Heck, Frey, if you'd open your eyes, you'd see how many guys are waiting for you to notice them."

Rupert's kindness warmed me. I'd never heard so many words come out of his mouth without offending me in some way.

As if Rupert realized the same thing and not wanting to tarnish his reputation as a womanizer, he ruined the moment. "All those other guys may be able to show you love and gooshy feelings, but I can show you one hell of a night. So if your lonely nights get too lonely, call me."

I smacked his arm with my clutch. "Why do you have to be such a creep? We were having a perfectly nice conversation, and you had to go and sully it."

"Call me if you get lonely," Rupert shouted, then sped away from me before I had the chance to smack him again.

❤

I woke on my couch and pulled dozens of tissues off my baby-doll nightgown. Last night, I avoided any more contact with Rupert by watching three of my favorite movies: *The Notebook*, *Say Anything*, and *Romeo and Juliet* with (swoon) Leonardo DiCaprio. I always cried in the opening credits of *The Notebook* because I knew the sadness to come, so by the time I made it to *Romeo and Juliet* I'd emptied a whole box of Kleenex.

Losing myself in fictional romance had always been a way I escaped from my own loneliness. I usually woke in the morning refreshed and back to my usual hopeless-romantic self.

Not that morning though. I stared at the pile of mascara-stained tissues on the ground and used my bunny slippers to shove them under the coffee table. Even that took more energy than I'd wanted to spend. If I could have, I'd have stayed in my pajamas all day, watching every Nicholas Sparks movie I owned.

My depressing attitude would've troubled me if I had enough time to reflect on it, but I was late.

As a general rule, I didn't fly in my apartment. I liked to pretend to be as normal as the humans down in the big city, but time wouldn't allow for such luxuries. I zipped into my bedroom, wings fluttering like a hummingbird, and pulled on the first dress I touched—a black halter-neck, circle dress with a sheer, black polka-dot overlay. It matched my mood perfectly—dark.

I pulled the sponge curlers out of my hair and did my best to arrange the locks around my face. They weren't cooperating, so I pulled them into a high ponytail, tacking on a red, fabric flower clip to dress it up.

Using my toaster for a mirror, I stroked on mascara while scarfing down a granola bar. Out of habit, I glanced at myself in my full-length mirror on the back of my front door. Without enough time to change anything anyway, I frowned at my rushed-looking appearance and headed toward the office.

"Oh good, I'm glad I'm not the only one running late," Mariah said, holding the door open to Cupid HQ. She looked like a hotter mess than I did. Her long, brown hair was slapped in a knot on top of her head, a far cry from the perfectly straight style she usually wore, but her hairstyle wasn't what made my jaw drop. She was wearing tight, dark wash jeans, paired with a crop-top with *Classy AF* written in swirling, glittery cursive. It was the same, not-so-classy shirt she'd worn yesterday. Someone like Mariah never wore the same clothes two days in a row.

I schooled my face when I realized I wasn't looking my best either. "I fell asleep on my couch and forgot to set an alarm." I touched my hair, wishing I would have used more hairspray.

She tugged at her wrinkled shirt.

"Do you think Daphne will notice we're so late?" I asked, changing the subject.

"Rupert said he'd distract her, so I can float by her and grab my own assignments. She'll think someone else helped us with our cards and be none the wiser," Mariah said, lowering her voice. "We do it all of the time. Daphne is so oblivious to everything as it is, and she hangs on Rupert's every word like some pathetic schoolgirl." She shivered. "She's like three times his age. It's so gross."

I didn't think it was all that gross. Daphne was a first-year supervisor, having just finished her Hundred a few months ago. Sure, she was technically one hundred and twenty, but she had the body of a twenty-year-old. The mindset of one, too.

"Hi." Mariah wiggled her fingers at Rupert as she floated past him at the circulation desk talking to Daphne, right where Mariah said he'd be.

Daphne sent annoyed glances our way. What had I done to deserve a look like that?

"Morning." Rupert bit his bottom lip as his eyes looked Mariah up and down. He had the decency to look ashamed when he saw me catch him. "And good morning, sunshine. Or should I say Moonlight Lady? What's with the black?"

I shrugged. "It's a black dress kind of day."

He flitted to my side, following me as I followed Mariah toward the assignment room. She looked back, eyeing how close he stood next to me.

I backed away from him, letting her know I wasn't encouraging him. "Aren't you supposed to be distracting Daphne?" I asked in a whisper. We'd put distance between our supervisor and us, but I knew the building carried voices.

A smug smile tugged at his lips. "I just gave her a nice thought to mull over. She'll be distracted for a minute or two."

Mariah looked back at us and threw up her Veil when Rupert gave her an encouraging nod. The door to the assignment room opened seemingly on its own.

Rupert body blocked me from following in after her before the door clicked closed. "I missed you last night," he said, leaning in close. "Why didn't you come get a drink?"

I held my breath so I wouldn't breathe in his cologne. I didn't need the heady feeling when I had rules to break. "Unlike some people, I don't feel the need to drink every night."

"I know you don't always get a drink, but you usually come hang out, at least for a little bit."

"I was busy."

"Busy stalking another Fated couple?"

"No," I said, even though that's what I should have been doing. I needed to figure out how to get my couple to Seal their Kiss. "I had a very interesting night. Did you wonder why I'm running late and my hair is less than perfect?" I asked, leading him to assume untrue, but more exciting theories than the truth.

He stood slack-jawed in front of me for longer than normal without speaking.

I recognized the instant he knew I was lying. He tossed his arm on the doorframe, and his dimple came out to play. "I kind of like your hair pulled up like that. I can see the mole I like so much." He grazed my beauty mark on my neck, with his thumb, then dropped his hand when I made a move to chomp on it with my teeth.

"You're feisty this morning." He laughed. "I like it."

"Please go distract Daphne so I can get in and out of here as soon as possible. Breaking the rules gives me heebie-jeebies."

He chucked me under the chin with a wink. "As you wish." His voice reminded me of Wesley form *The Princess Bride*. That was the second time in two days he'd referenced a classic love movie. Maybe he had a romantic bone somewhere in that gorgeous body of his after all.

I took Daphne's over-the-top giggle as the sign I needed

that she was giving Rupert her undivided attention, so I Veiled myself and slipped into the assignment room. We were strongly discouraged from Veiling ourselves while in Paver's Cloud, though they couldn't keep us from doing it. I didn't want to get caught sneaking around though so I indulged in the taboo.

Just after I'd made it inside, the door swung open and shut with no visible hand guiding it, so I assumed it was Mariah leaving, Veiled as well.

Alone and not quite sure what I was doing, I looked at the huge walls and tried to figure out where I was supposed to be looking. Library-catalogue styled drawers covered the walls, each one labeled with a letter, alphabetized by person.

How did I know which one to grab?

I cursed Rupert for keeping me from following Mariah in here on time; she would've been able to help me.

I scanned the drawers. There had to be millions of names.

One of them was mine.

I looked to the Ds, knowing my name was in one of those drawers. That was a dangerous line of thinking, so I dragged my eyes away.

I searched for something indicating which cards I was assigned. I'd almost given up and turned myself in when I saw a row of baskets with the name of a serving Cupid on each.

I located mine, third from the top, between two of my sisters: Damara and Isis Darling. My third sister, Lada, was after Isis, the four Darling sisters right in a row. My and Rupert's baskets were the only ones left with cards still in them. I pulled my two assignment cards out and opened them, waiting for either Daphne or Rupert to open the door, so I didn't have to risk being caught sneaking out of here, Veiled.

The girl was Carrie Timms—a cute blonde with a friendly smile. She worked at a boutique furniture store in Denton, went to school at the University of North Texas, and lived right around the corner from her job.

The boy, Adam Hannon, was so handsome I stared way longer than was necessary. Even from the mugshot-like picture, I could tell he was strong. His jawline was etched into a perfect square, and his shoulders took up most of the picture. He had sun-kissed hair and ocean-blue eyes. He wasn't smiling, but I could tell he was sweet based on the natural up-turn of his lips.

I hoped my Fated looked like him.

My eyes darted back to the drawer I knew housed my Fate card, heart thudding in my chest. If I just took a peak, I could find him on my own and not have to wait for Cupid's Kiss. That couldn't harm anything, could it?

Not if I'd ended up with him anyway.

I looked back at Adam's picture and felt a longing to love someone like him.

Before I'd fully made up my mind, I was flying to the catalogue.

I pulled out the drawer labeled De-Di and skimmed through the cards, finding the one labeled Darling, Freya.

Just a peek, I promised myself.

Chapter Five

$\mathscr{I}$ had my fingernail under the heart-shaped seal, ready to open it when I heard Rupert's and Daphne's laughs flood the room. I held my breath.

Daphne got dangerously close to me, and I thought I was caught, but all she did was slam the open De-Di drawer closed.

"I was in a hurry this morning," she said to Rupert, excusing the drawer being left open. "So, about what you said earlier," she purred, stretching her hands to Rupert's collar and straightening it even though it had been starched and wasn't out of place.

"Yes, about what I said earlier ..." He pulled her closer to him and rubbed his hand down her back.

She wiggled her way even closer, smashing her body against his.

Afraid of being stuck in here, forced to witness Rupert take Daphne for a test ride, I risked the exposure and dropped my Veil long enough for Rupert to see I was still in the room. I raised it again, shielding me from sight.

Rupert coughed in surprise and gently put space between them. "Maybe we should do what I was talking about later, I'm getting a late start this morning. You know how I late working late."

Daphne unwrapped her hands from his neck. "You sure know how to drive a woman crazy."

"It's half the fun." He winked. "Oh, was that the phone?"

"Was it?" Daphne angled her ear toward the door. "Linda will get it. It's probably Lada needing directions. All four of those Darling girls are so air-headed."

I straightened. Did she really say that?

"Not all of them," Rupert said, tucking a hair behind her ear. "Freya's not so bad."

I nodded in appreciation even though he could no longer see me.

"Are you kidding? She's the worst. She may not call and ask me stupid questions all time like her sisters, but she's like a little girl still upstairs." Daphne tapped on her head with an index finger. "She's always so happy. Someone needs to teach her that the world isn't so great."

"She might be a little naïve," Rupert reluctantly agreed. "But—"

Daphne cut him off. "A lot naïve."

"There's the phone again, someone must really need you."

"Ugh, fine. Grab your card." She nodded to the basket. "Don't tell anyone I let you be in here alone." She gave him a long, yearning look before she closed the door behind her.

"Come out, come out, wherever you are." Rupert spread his hand out flat above his eyes as if looking for something far out in the distance.

I shoved my card, along with Adam and Carrie's cards, into my purse. There was no way I could get mine back in its drawer without Rupert catching me.

Dropping the Veil, I said, "I'm right here. But I'm going to have to Veil myself anyway when we leave. She can't know I was in here."

"That's true," he admitted, "but we might as well take advantage of the privacy as long as we have it." He moved toward me like a panther.

"Ew." I Veiled myself again, not liking the way he was looking at me. I flew over and grabbed his card out of the box. I could see it perfectly fine, but I knew that to Rupert, the card turned invisible the second I touched it. He grunted as I shoved the card hard against his stomach.

"You like it rough? I would've pegged you for a sweet and slow kind of girl, but if you like it rough, I'd be willing to change it up and try it out for you." He laughed, trying to find where I was.

If he'd been able to hear me, I would've told him what he could do to himself, but as it was, I had to communicate through physical means. I pinched his earlobe and dragged him toward the door. His wings were tucked, so he was forced to stand on his tip toes like a little boy.

"Ow, watch it." But he got the hint and opened the door.

I stayed close to him so the door didn't hit me on its closing swing.

He was much taller than me, probably over six feet, and his back was long and lean. I wondered how many girls had seen his strong back without his shirt on. Then I wondered what he meant by willing to give "it" a try, referring to a rough style, instead of a slow and sweet style. Did he mean that he was usually a slow and sweet type?

That surprised me. Admittedly, I'd never thought of how he'd be at all, but being forced to think about it, I wouldn't have assumed he'd be sensual.

"Break room," Rupert said, barely a whisper.

Following his lead, I followed him down the long hallway in the direction of the break room. Each of the Pavers' Headquarters backed up to the room, allowing us to mingle together, Paver teambuilding and all that. Before a shift or between doubles, the room was filled with Oracles, Elves, Sprites, and Cupids who came together and bonded over coffee and muffins. Being that it was late morning, the only people I had to worry about stumbling across were HQ staff taking a break.

We were lucky. The room was empty. After giving a thorough inspection of the place, I appeared to him. "Thanks for covering for me," I said, heading to the door.

"Wait. You owe me," he said, striding toward the coffee pot. Rupert used his wings less than any Paver I knew. It was almost like he wished he was a normal human. Like me.

"I said thank you."

"I know you said thank you but sit and have a cup of coffee to show me your thanks."

Not wanting to owe him a favor, I grudgingly sat at the white plastic table and accepted the mug from his outstretched hand. I hadn't met Lana for our usual cup this morning, so I was in need of caffeine.

"Are you going to tell me why you were late this morning,

young lady? And don't give me that BS about doing something interesting. I know you better than that."

I sighed. "I fell asleep on my couch and didn't set my alarm."

"Watching re-runs of *The Bachelor*?"

"No." I wrinkled my nose. "I don't like reality TV. It shows the worst of people. I watched a couple of movies, nothing exciting." Fiddling with a stirring straw, I said, "I know you had an exciting night."

He grinned. "That I did. Where are your assignments today? Maybe we can tag-team. You get both of the boys, and I'll get both of the girls." He opened his cards and read them. "Downtown Fort Worth and Haslet."

"No, but thanks. I actually get to know my assignments and take an interest in them." Adam's picture flashed in my mind. "Besides, we're not supposed to do that. You can seriously screw up a match that way." I bit my lip. "How would that even work?"

"I Kiss my first girl, you Kiss your first guy, then we Kiss, swapping assignments, and then I Kiss the second girl and you Kiss the second guy."

"Like I said—no."

He shrugged. "What about lunch?"

"Mine are in Denton, far away from yours. You're already getting coffee. Don't get greedy."

"You're right. I'm surprised you accepted."

"Me too." I walked to the coffee pot and grabbed a to-go cup, dumped the remainder of my coffee inside, and topped it off. "Want a cup for the flight?"

He waved his hand, dismissing the cup. "Dinner?"

The door from the Oracle office opened, and Marisol, one of the kindest souls I'd ever met, flew into the room. She lived across the hall from me, and always managed to say exactly what I needed to hear. Oracles were wise like that. I wondered when that particular character trait kicked in. Jacqueline was still waiting for hers.

"Good morning, Marisol," I said, ignoring Rupert's question.

"Hello, honey. Is it still morning?" She glanced at the clock on the microwave. "I guess that means I can have one more cup of coffee." She shot me a naughty grin. "Just don't tell Brittney. That girl watches my blood pressure closer than my doctor."

"She just loves you," I said, pouring a cup for her.

"She needs to love someone else. You don't think you could help an old lady and fix her up, do you?"

"Sure thing." Rupert inserted himself between us. "Like I was saying, there's a great Mexican place in Flower Mound, half way between Denton and Fort Worth."

I stared at him in awe. "Rupert Lovett, are you asking a girl on a real date? Not just to your bedroom?" I turned to Marisol. "You heard him, right? I didn't invent it."

She nodded behind her coffee, taking in a slow satisfied gulp.

A smug smile crept onto his features. "Well, the hope is that we'll end up in the bedroom."

Marisol choked on her sip.

"Then no," I said, securing the lid on my cup. "I don't want to owe you anything."

"Fine, it's not a date. No expectations. I promise not to even hint at expectations, just two co-workers having a meal after work."

"Still gonna have to say no. I know what goes on in that disgusting mind of yours."

"Freya, come on. I know how much you love being down there. I do too. None of the other Pavers get it." Rupert took the coffee from my hands and slipped a sleeve over the hot cup. "There's life down there, strangers everywhere you look. We can blend in and be like everyone else. We can be anyone else." There was sincere longing in his eyes.

I teetered on the edge of accepting, and his thick eyebrows raised in hope.

Behind Rupert, Marisol nodded. "If you don't go, I will."

Two against one. No fair. I groaned, already knowing I was going to regret it. "Fine, but if you say one thing—"

He cut me off, "I won't."

"Put one hand on me—"

"They'll stay in my lap." He put his hands in his lap,

showing me he was able.

"Even so much as look at me in a way that makes me think that you're picturing me naked—"

"I'll wear sunglasses." A smile broke his face apart.

I smiled too. "I mean it, if I feel like you're treating it like a date, I walk."

"Deal." He extended his hand.

I ignored it. "I'll meet you there at eight."

"I'll be waiting."

"Waiting for what?" Daphne asked, walking into the breakroom. "No one was on the phone."

I left the room without responding, conscious of Rupert's eyes on me the whole walk out the door.

What have I gotten myself into?

Chapter Six

The door to the boutique Carrie Timms worked at chimed as I walked in.

"Hey, how are you?" Carrie said from the back of the store. Her southern twang was thicker than most that live close to Dallas.

"Good, yourself?"

Carrie was sanding an old dresser, elbow-deep in turpentine and wood dust, smiling. "Fantastic. How can I help you?"

She stood to greet me, wiping her hands off on a pair of worn overalls with hand painted daisies scattered about the fabric. Her dark blond hair was pulled into a messy bun on the side of her head.

I shewed her away. "Don't get up. I'm window shopping."

"All right, well let me know if there's anything I can help you with."

I looked around the place, absolutely in love with the shabby-chic furniture the store offered. My entire apartment was decorated the same way. Unfortunately, there was only one furniture store in Paver's Cloud, so I had the same furniture as anyone else with my taste.

"See anything you like?"

"Everything," I said, running my hand over a distressed-yellow side table. "Do you make it all yourself?"

"Just a few things. I'm working on more. This dresser will be my first large piece when I finish. I'm still learning a lot. That's mine over there." Carrie pointed to an old, brown and red bread box. "That too." She used her foot to indicate a blue door-wedge with tiny, gold loops swirling all over.

Who would have thought to embellish a triangular piece of scrap wood?

"This one I'm the proudest of." She walked me over to the far wall and pulled a large, wooden picture frame off the wall.

"Oh wow, I love it. My whole apartment is decorated in that distressed eggshell."

"You wanna be my first customer?" She looked at me with big, impossible-to-deny eyes.

"I don't really have a way of getting it home," I said, imagining myself carrying a wooden square almost as big as me, while flying.

"You can keep it here 'til you're done walking the square," she offered.

"What the heck," I agreed. Maybe I'd be able to talk Rupert into carrying it for me.

"Really?" She jumped, clapping like a little kid.

How could I change my mind after that show of elation? "Yes, really. I have a couple more stops before I head home, you can keep it until about six?"

"Sure can. We don't close till seven."

I paid her for the picture frame before I strolled out the door. I took a lap around the Denton Square, and when I was sure no one was paying attention to me, I Veiled myself then made a beeline for the back of Carrie's store. I'd noticed while I was in there that Carrie had the back door propped open to let the turpentine fumes escape.

I crossed my fingers that the door was still open so I could slip inside. Luck was on my side.

I lingered above Carrie, watching each meticulous move. She made stripping wood look like an art form. When she pulled her head away from her work to stretch her neck, I swooped in and gave her a quick Cupid's Kiss. The pink sparkles from the connection danced from her lips, telling me the job was done, and I disappeared the way I came.

That was a girl I was happy to help, I thought, as I zoomed above the busy streets of Denton. She was happy with herself and was making the life she wanted happen. If there was anyone who deserved the handsome guy she was paired with, it was her.

I told myself that, because it was time for me to go see Adam Holden, the boy with the blue eyes and sun-kissed hair from the picture that made me catch my breath.

They were even more perfect for each other, I realized when I read that he was a finishing carpenter at a popular home-building company. He'd know how to build her wonderful pieces of furniture, and she'd be able to dress them up beautifully. I saw a small business in their future.

Suppressing the spike of jealousy, I pulled out my cell phone and routed my way to Adam's house.

A number one hovered over my text message icon. Upon further inspection, I saw it was a text from Rupert, containing the address to the restaurant followed by a winking emoticon. I tried to suppress a smile and ignore the excited sunshine in my chest. The rational part of me knew dinner was just another attempt to get me in his bed, but the hopeless-romantic part of me wondered if I was the girl to get him to change his ways.

I sent him a short response, "See you at eight," then tried to remember what it was I grabbed my phone for in the first place. Oh yes, Adam—a harmless yet equally beautiful man to concentrate on.

Chapter Seven

$\mathcal{I}$ found Adam lounging with his dog on a hammock in his back yard. Could he seriously be any cuter?

Of course, I'd have to remain Veiled for my meeting with him—I couldn't barge into his backyard, although I'd love to have a nice long conversation with him. I should have dived down and planted Cupid's Kiss him right away. Instead, I found a nice seat in one of the trees his hammock was hanging from to watch him doze.

His red Irish Setter lifted its head off his lap and looked about. The dog voiced a protective rumble from its throat, not sure what it was protecting its owner from.

"Easy Ruby," Adam said. His gentle and deep voice carried itself to my perch in the tree. If I didn't have wings to keep me airborne, I would've literally fallen for him right then.

Still not convinced they were alone, Ruby jumped off the hammock to search for the mystery presence. Her leap caught Adam off-guard, and the hammock rotated, spitting him out onto the ground.

"Oh, you little rascal!" Pulling himself to his knees, he sprang at Ruby, tackling her into a playful roll on the ground.

She barked, inching close to the ground, preparing to retaliate.

Adam on all fours, and Ruby on her hind legs, their wrestle looked like a dance, him laughing and her growling. With a mighty push, Ruby tackled Adam onto his back, and she pawed at him and covered his face with kisses.

"Stop it. Stop it," Adam said through chuckles. Finding a

knotted rope on the ground next to his hand, he picked it up and showed it to Ruby. He threw it across the yard. "Fetch!"

The rope landed against the fence in a muddy strip of land lower than the rest of yard. Ruby ran straight into the mud, coating herself in dirty water. Something apparently smelled interesting because she nosedived in and rolled, matting her fur even more with sludge.

"Oh no." Adam covered his face with his hands, shaking his head. "Come here, Ruby."

Ruby pranced over to Adam, obeying her master.

"What did I tell you about rolling in the mud?"

Ruby dropped the rope she'd retrieved, hung her head, and whined.

Adam straightened from his punishing stance and pouted his bottom lip. "I hate yelling as much as you hate being yelled at."

She lowered herself submissively to the ground.

"Well come on, get up."

He picked up the dropped rope and threw it. Once again, it landed in the puddle by the fence. Ruby refrained from rolling, though I saw her physical need to do so.

They played fetch until Ruby panted heavily. At which point, Adam unwound the hose and caught Ruby off guard with a line of water hitting her on the back. Excited, she turned to face the water and chomped at the stream with her teeth.

"Okay, okay, let's get serious." Adam pinched the hose, stopping the water from flowing. "Come sit." He pointed to the concrete porch and pulled a bottle of shampoo from a plastic bucket next to the hose.

He'd taken too long to begin the bathing process. Ruby shook her body vigorously, launching water and mud all over Adam.

Using the back of his hand, he wiped the brown, clumpy liquid from his face and groaned. "I should've seen that coming."

Dropping the hose, letting the water flow into the grass, Adam unbuttoned his dirty shirt and tossed it to the ground. His wet, sculpted arms and chest reflected the sun like celestial beams.

Like a bee to a flower, I found I'd flown off my perch and was headed toward him, hand out ready to run my fingers down his washboard abs.

"Oh my!" I blurted. Shifting into reverse, I flew away from him as fast as I could. It wasn't until I was out of his yard and two houses over that I trusted myself to come to a stop.

What had I almost done? The memory of his gorgeousness took over my body, and my wings propelled me back toward the house without my permission.

"Get a grip, Freya! He's just a boy. Well, a man," I corrected myself. "Regardless of his manliness, he's not your man. He's Carrie's. You like Carrie, remember? Anyway, it doesn't matter. He is Fated to be with someone else. Even if you fell in love with him and convinced him to fall in love with you, it would only end in heartache because he's Fated to Carrie. And you will be Fated to someone else."

My monologue trailed off because I remembered my very own assignment card was sitting in my purse. Looking around—why? I didn't know, I was Veiled—I slowly and carefully opened my purse and saw the card with my name written in silver cursive on the front. I exhaled, looked around once more and extended my hand into my purse.

My phone blared to life with the chorus of *At Last* by Etta James. I pushed the sacred assignment card to the side and grabbed the phone. Lana's face was on the screen.

"What's up?"

"Hello to you, too."

"Sorry. Hey, Lana. What's up?"

"What happened to you this morning? I waited around at the coffee shop forever."

I pressed my hand to forehead. "I'm so sorry. I woke up late, and then Rupert cornered me in the break room."

"What did he want?"

Deciding not to tell her about the not-date that I have with Rupert later, I told her another version of the truth. "The same thing he always wants."

"Did you do what I said? Start talking wedding dates and all of that? Maybe you should mention babies, too—twins!"

"No, ha ha." Though, I reminded myself to say that if he got weird at dinner.

"I was just making sure you didn't fall in your closet and were swallowed by petticoats and polka-dots."

"Very funny, Miss I Wear Five Pounds of Jewelry Every Day. No, I'm not in my closet sinking into a sea of dresses. I'm on an assignment."

"Me too. I'll let you go and see you tonight."

"Actually ..." I hesitated, "Actually, I have plans after work." I grimaced, knowing I wouldn't be able to get off the phone until I told her what plans I had.

"Plans?" she asked, surprised. "With who?"

I didn't answer, hoping my shameful silence would explain for me and I wouldn't have to voice the truth. I didn't want her to hear the excitement in my tone if I had to physically say I was going to dinner with Rupert aloud. Because if I was honest with myself, I was excited.

"Who do you have plans with?" she pressed.

I swallowed hard.

"Don't tell me you've finally crossed over the line and are going out with an assignment. Damn it, Freya, you'll get your Veil and Kiss revoked."

"I'm not stupid. And what do you mean 'finally?' Do you actually expect me to do that?" My eyes zeroed in on the top of Adam's house, and I began flying toward his yard on autopilot.

"Well, maybe. I don't know. I wouldn't be surprised. But that's beside the point. Who do you have plans with?"

"I gotta go. Adam's heading into the house, and I have to make it in before he closes the door."

"Adam? Your assignment? That's what I mean, calling your assignments by their first—"

I pressed the end button on the phone before Lana finished. She was right, and I didn't want to hear it. It wasn't expressly forbidden to refer to assignment by name, but there was really no reason to get so attached that it was necessary to refer to them at all.

Adam disappeared into his house, and Ruby followed him.

"Dag nab it!" I zoomed toward the door, trying to make it inside before Adam shut it behind Ruby.

The rush was unnecessary. He left the back door wide open,

allowing Ruby to come and go as she pleased.

When I entered his house, Ruby ran over and smelled the air around me. I was careful to float above her so I wouldn't graze her by accident, but I wanted to pet her.

I hadn't thought about what Adam's house would like on the inside, but if I had, I imagined it would have been exactly like what I found. The white walls were mostly bare, save for a clock and a framed painting of horses on a pasture. His television took up most of the living room wall, a leather sofa sat across from it aimed right at the TV. There were no rugs or knickknacks anywhere to personalize the home.

I followed Adam to a basic bedroom, white walls, an unmade queen bed with a plain blue comforter tossed to one side of the bed, and another enormous television. This was the perfect blank canvas for Carrie, I thought, shoving down a pang of jealousy.

I lost myself in thoughts of what it'd be like if I were in Carrie's shoes and only snapped out of my self-pity when I saw Adam head to the bathroom, unzipping his pants on the way.

I scurried out of the room and made myself comfortable on his couch while I waited for him to shower off the mess Ruby had splashed on him. Careful to listen for the water to turn off, I picked up a leather journal resting on an end table.

The book was filled with sketches of shelves, tables, lawn chairs, and even full kitchens—cabinets, islands, and pantries. I sat the book down where I found it when I heard the water turn off in the shower. Snuggling deeper into the sofa while I waited for him, I daydreamed about a house he'd design, and we'd live in together.

We'd have two boys and then a girl, so the boys could protect her when she got older. Accounting for his last name, Hannon, I had already named our first boy, Billy, our daughter, Addley, and was deciding between Matthew or Christopher for our second son when the smell of men's body wash filled the room.

Acting as if he'd caught me fantasizing about a life I knew we'd never have, I sprang from the couch. Good thing, too, because Adam plopped onto the same spot I'd been sitting.

His eyes looked straight through me and onto the television screen, turning it on with a remote he'd dug out of the couch cushions.

I made myself comfortable on the opposite side of the couch and drifted off to sleep while watching him watch *Cops* on the flat screen.

I opened my eyes when the sun was low in the sky and found that Adam, too, had fallen asleep. He was so beautiful. His lashes were long and curled up as they made contact with his skin. His skin was tanned by the sun, and I counted six dark, round freckles on the right side of his face. Curious about the other side, I sat straighter to extend my wings and flit to his left side, but Ruby groaned and pawed at me to stay still.

She'd fallen asleep, and her head sat in my lap, comfortable and content.

Not seeing the harm in petting her since she'd obviously accepted that while invisible, I was still worthy of her love, I scooped one of her big floppy ears into my hand and massaged her.

Her tail slowly bounced on the couch.

Adam shifted his weight, trying to find another comfortable position. With his eyes still closed he caught her tail and wagged his hand along with her. "Happy girl." His voice cut through the air.

She turned her head toward him then her body followed.

I used this opportunity to stand from the couch and collect myself. I really should get going. Lana would wonder what was taking me so long to get back home.

That's when it hit me. I wasn't going to be late to meet Lana, I was going to be late to meet Rupert. My eyes flashed to the cable box under Adam's TV. It was already seven forty-five. I only had fifteen minutes to fly from Denton to Flower Mound to meet Rupert for dinner.

I shot Rupert a text, telling him I was on my way, but running late.

Chapter Eight

"There's my girl," Rupert said, draping an arm over my shoulder.

Before I responded, I used my thumb and forefinger to drop his hand. I wouldn't get comfortable, I promised myself. "You could have gotten a table."

"And miss the chance at making my grand entrance with a looker like you? I think not." His eyes roamed up and down my figure appreciatively.

"Where are your sunglasses?" I said, reminding him of his promise to not look at me like he had x-ray vision.

"Forgot them," he said, dismissing my comment. "You can even make flying-hair look good."

My hands groped at the mess on top of my head, and I stopped walking long enough to refasten my hair into its holder.

He caught my hand that was trying to re-pin the red flower onto the top of my ponytail. He pinned it to the halter strap of my dress instead. "I wasn't trying to make you self-conscious. I really meant that you look good."

I stammered for the words "thank you," caught off-guard by his sincerity.

"All the guys in here would've wondered what it was that made your hair look that way." He winked.

"Ugh. I knew that compliment was too good to be true. You always find a way to make everything go back to … well you know."

"Sex?" he asked mischievously.

"Yeah, that."

"You can say it, you know. It's not a dirty word. Try it on

for size. Ssseeexx." He dragged the last word out like a snake hiss, his mouth so very close to my ear.

My body warmed at the proximity and at the embarrassment of the word.

"Welcome to Cristina's. How are y'all?" the perky hostess asked us.

"We're good. Yourself?" Rupert answered, leaving me to cool down.

"I'm great, thank you for asking. You'd be surprised how many people don't bother asking me how I am."

"Really? That's a shame." Rupert leaned in, laying his lady-killer grin on her. "How long is the wait for two?"

I looked around the restaurant for the first time and saw people overflowing at the long bar, little black boxes with red flashing lights in their hands.

"Only about fifteen minutes." She giggled. "What's your name? I'll put you on the list."

"Rhett," he told her, "Rhett Butler."

My eyes widened at the *Gone with the Wind* alias. "Are you serious?" I asked him after the hostess handed him the pager, and we walked toward the bar.

"As a heart attack. I'm suave. I'm debonair. I need a name that matches who I am. Rupert" —he frowned— "is a monstrosity. I don't know what I could have done to my mother before I was even born to make her hate me so."

I laughed even though I liked his name. "But why Rhett Butler?" I was trying hard not let on how much I approved of his taste. "It's so iconic, people have to recognize it as made up."

"You're one to talk, Mrs. Juliet Capulet." His eyebrows raised, knowingly.

I tongued the inside of my mouth while I try to think of something to say. "It's Julie; people have to try really hard to make the connection. How do you know that anyway?"

He shrugged and turned his attention to the bartender. "Two Top Shelf Frozen Margaritas, please."

"No, I don't need a margarita," I protested.

"You do need a margarita. These are to die for."

"No, I don't." But my arguing had gotten me nowhere.

Rupert fished my ID out of my purse and showed it to the bartender. A moment later, Rupert passed me a goblet-shaped glass filled with frozen heaven. He wasn't wrong, one sip and I knew it was the best margarita I'd ever tasted.

"How did you know I have an ID?" I asked him while walking to our table.

The smitten hostess personally guided us to a booth. Once seated, she handed me a menu, but glided one into Rupert's hands, making eye contact the whole time.

"Julio will be right with you," she said to Rupert and slowly walked away from us, swinging her hips more than necessary.

I snapped my fingers in front of Rupert's eyes. "Gross, she is like eighteen."

"So, I'm only twenty-one."

"Um no, you're twenty-seven."

"My mind might be too old for her, but my body is the perfect age."

I tisked, even though it had been earlier that same day when I'd made that very argument for Daphne,

"How did you know I have an ID?" I asked again.

"Cause you're like me, babe. You can't stand staying hidden behind the Veil. We take every chance we can get to live out here with the rest of them. How else did you think I knew about this place?"

I nodded. He wasn't wrong. I'd received my Driver's License as soon as I started my Hundred. I'd used one of my assignments as an excuse to get Cupid HQ to make me one, saying that I was having a hard time Sealing the Kiss with a couple and wanted to 'meet them' at a club and play matchmaker in person. The license had gotten me into the club without problems, but I'd only used it for access into bars and clubs or to order drinks but had never driven.

Julio, a handsome man with cute black-rimmed glasses, came to take our order. Rupert, or should I say Rhett, insisted we order their table-side guacamole as an appetizer, I chose my own dinner plate. I selected a chicken plate while he ordered something I couldn't pronounce and didn't recognize.

We made surprisingly pleasant conversation as we ate guacamole and waited for the main course. He told me about his favorite places around the Metroplex: An Irish pub in Addison called Sherlock's, Louie Louie's Dueling Piano Bar in Arlington, and Cloud Nine, the restaurant in the Reunion Tower in Downtown Dallas. I'd heard of the places he mentioned but had never been to them myself.

"Did your assignments work there?" I asked. "I never get cool places like that." The most exciting place I'd gone to because of an assignment was Billy Bob's in Fort Worth. I'd made excuses to go there a couple of times without an assignment too.

"No, I get most of my assignments done before lunch then hit the streets looking for action."

"Oh right. You don't see the point in spending time with your couples. I forgot."

"Pollo a la Stephie for you." Julio set a delicious looking meal in front of me, interrupting our conversation before it took a turn for the worse. "And for you sir, La Gran Parrilliada de Guadalajara." The server proceeded to place a pound of meat on a raised metal plate with a flame underneath it, a side dish complete with all the standard Mexican dish trimmings, an empty plate for him to build his tacos, and tortilla holder onto the table. Rupert's cornucopia took up most of the table.

"Is everything you do this ostentatious?" I asked.

Rupert pondered seriously for a moment then gave me one sharp nod. "Yes."

"You are unbelievable." I shook my head.

"That's not the first time I've been told that." He pointed his fork at me and winked.

I felt color rising to my cheeks. I hated that he made me think of … stuff … so often. "That is not what I meant. And you're supposed to be on your best behavior tonight, remember?"

"Oh, I promise you, I am on my best behavior." He flashed me a suggestive grin then dove into his food. He could even make eating messy tacos look good.

I wanted to say something disapproving back at him, but I found myself staring at him. Sometimes, his stupid smile stole every thought in mind, every breath in my body.

"Everything okay with your food?" he asked, concerned.

"It's fine." I took a bite of delicious chicken and found

spinach hiding inside. "How were your assignments today?"

"They were good. I took a page out of your rule book and actually took the time to get to know the couple."

"You did?" Maybe there was hope for him to change after all.

"Mmhmm," he hummed, still chewing. "The guy works at a lube and tube, funny dude, a real life of the party. And she's a single mother, raising a three-year-old alone. I think they'll be good for each other. He'll make her laugh and lift some of her burdens, and she'll help him grow up and give him a focal point for his love. He is kind of a womanizer—the scoundrel," Rupert said, mock-horrified.

"What a scoundrel." I shook my head, but I felt the corners of my mouth lift.

"How was your day? Fall in love with love again? Yesterday was a bad day for you."

"Maybe."

More like fell in love with my assignment.

Then I decided to give Rupert a taste of his own medicine and show him he wasn't the only handsome man in existence, the same way he flaunted all his girls in my face. I was ashamed at how much the jealousy was getting to me, but not ashamed enough to stop me. "Adam, my assignment, is very handsome. Strong. Burly. Blond. And he works with his hands."

I looked at Rupert in hopes of seeing jealousy twinkling in his eyes, but he was only eating his food and nodding along, so I continued. "He has this dog, Ruby, and she's super sweet. And it was so funny." I laughed, cutting another slice of chicken. "She splashed mud all over him, so he had to take his shirt off right in the middle of the yard."

Rupert's eyebrow flicked, but he didn't say anything. I started talking about Carrie, so I wouldn't accidentally tell Rupert I had a hard time keeping my hands to myself. "Carrie is his Fated. She works in a boutique furniture store off the square in Denton. Anyway, I bought this picture frame from her." My smile faded. "Darn it. I forgot to pick it up because I was running late to get here."

"I like dogs too," Rupert said, bringing the attention back to his favorite topic—himself.

"Really?" I put my fork down. "I said all of that, and all you have to say is that you like dogs too?"

"Well, you clearly have a crush on this guy, and I'm not burly or blond or work with my hands, so I can't compete there. But I am handsome, which you already know. And I love dogs. Something you didn't know. I just have to make sure I'm still in the running for your heart."

The mention of my heart out of Rupert's mouth made it speed its beat. "My heart? I thought you were only in the running for my body."

"I reckon I won't get one without the other."

I chewed on that thought as I finished my dinner. I wondered if what Percy, Penny, and Lana had been saying was true. Could Rupert actually love me? If not today, was it possible he could grow to love me if I gave him the chance?

It was too risky to let myself think about it. Because I knew if I allowed myself believe he was sincere, I'd fall so hard for him.

When the time came, I insisted on paying my share of the tab.

"The man is supposed to pay." Rupert pulled the check the server had divided for me out of my hands.

"This isn't the fifties. But even if it was, the man is supposed to pay on a date. We are not on a date," I reminded him, snatching the bill from his fingers.

"Ow!" Rupert pulled his hand to his mouth, his full lips sucking at the fleshy part of his hand at the crease of his thumb. "You gave me a paper cut."

I sucked air into my mouth through clenched teeth. I loathed paper cuts. "I'm sorry," I said with true regret. "Let me see it."

Rupert pulled his hand from his mouth and extended it toward me. "Kiss it and make it feel better?" he asked hopefully, once his hand was in mine.

"I don't feel that bad," I said playfully, dropping his hand. It thudded onto the table. I reached for the check I'd let go of in exchange for his hand, but it was missing. My eyes narrowed at Rupert. "You cheated!"

"Don't hate the player, hate the game." Rupert chuckled.

"I have room in my heart to hate both."

Rupert's playful smile turned to a lazy, distracted one. "I know, Freya, you have so much room in that big heart of yours." His hand brushed hesitantly against mine as if he couldn't decide whether he wanted to grab it.

I couldn't decide what I wanted him to do either. Every time he used my name, my witty retorts fell away. His voice wasn't deep and crisp like Adam's, but it was pleasant in its own right—strong and confident, with a gravely quality to it when he was vulnerable.

Who was I kidding? Rupert was never vulnerable. He only pretended to be, so I'd let my guard down and be more susceptible to his charm. *Try again, Rupert, this chick is not falling for your tricks.*

I shifted purposefully against the booth's cushion and crossed my arms over my chest. "I want kids. Loads of them. How about you?" I followed Lana's advice.

"Four." Rupert didn't miss a beat but took on the same defensive body language I was using. "Two boys and two girls, in that order."

"Four?" My eyes widened.

"Yep, and I want them soon, so I can spend as much time with them as possible. I don't want to wait until my Hundred is over like my parents did. I want to be there for everything."

That surprised me more than the number. "You'd give up your life of parties and girls to raise kids?"

"That's why I'm getting it all out of my system now. I don't want to ever wish I'd done more. I don't want to resent them."

I was puzzled. I'd always thought of Rupert as a dog, and he was of course, but I was surprised to find he was more than that too. Lana's plan seemed to be backfiring. Rupert wasn't afraid of commitment. In fact, he was saying he's ready to jump head first into commitment.

He leaned forward, planting his crossed arms onto the table, his body extending over them toward me. "Why did you bring up kids?"

Afraid that if I weren't honest with him, he'd assume I was thinking about having kids with him, I said, "I was trying to scare you."

"Scare me? Why would you want to do that?"

"So you'd finally quit toying with me and leave me alone. I'm not one of those girls you chew up and spit out."

"I know exactly who you are, Freya." There was no mockery in his tone. No trickery and no games. He was looking past my face and into my soul.

And for the first time, I wanted him to see it.

A shiver ran up my spine. I hugged myself tighter and leaned into him. "I have no idea who you are."

His face froze, brow up, mid-smile. "Oh, come on, yes you do." His posture relaxed back into the booth, and that annoying cocky grin eclipsed his sincere expression. "I'm a player who knows what to say to get you in bed."

I flinched.

"Did it work?" he asked coolly. "Are you ready to let me ravish you?"

"That's what this was the whole time, wasn't it, another play to get me into your bed?" I swallowed a thick wad of rage, and something else, hurt? I stood and left the table without saying another word.

Tears stung my eyes.

That was when I realized that I'd believed him. For that tiny moment, I had imagined what our kids would like, all four of them with his dark hair and my green eyes. The girls in dresses and bows, the boys dressed like little men in Polos like their daddy.

Saltwater landed on my lips, and I tasted it as I bit my bottom lip to keep from bursting into tears before I make it outside where I could Veil myself.

♥

That night I laid in bed crying, cursing myself for agreeing to go out on that stupid not-date with Rupert. I'd refrained from dating perfectly nice Pavers all to avoid the feeling I had in my chest.

How could I have been so stupid? Of all the guys to take the chance on, why did I let it be Rupert? Shallow, conceded, womanizing Rupert.

Chapter Nine

$\mathcal{L}$ana let herself into my apartment in the morning. She carried coffee and donuts. She didn't ask me how I was doing and didn't tell me to get up. She settled into my bed, pulling the covers over her. She brought my head into her lap and stroked my hair until I fell back asleep.

I woke again later, not knowing how much time had passed but I knew it is well into the workday.

"What are you doing?" I asked, righting myself into a sitting position. Lana was on episode three of *Felicity*.

"Finally watching this show. I hate to admit it's really good. But why would Felicity move across the country to be with a boy she barely knows? And who is she talking to on that tape recorder?"

"She follows him 'cause she's a stupid girl, and she believes in stupid love. And you have to wait till the end to find out who she's talking to."

Lana looked at me with pity in her eyes. "Don't say that about love. You're in love with love."

"Correction: I was in love with love. Now I see it for what it is. An illusion."

My best friend squared her shoulders and looked me in the eyes. "I'm gonna kill him."

"What? No. He didn't do anything but be exactly who I know he is." Then after a moment of thinking, "How did you know? How did you know you were going to find me like this?" I reached for the bag of donuts Lana had on her side of the bed, and she shoved room-temperature coffee at me.

"When you hung up on me yesterday without telling

me who you had plans with, I connected the dots. You had coffee with him yesterday morning, and suddenly you had mysterious plans. I called him to verify my suspicions. He came to the Parched Paver last night and got piss-ass drunk and rambled about how he made you cry and—"

"He did what?" I shouted. I'd been so careful to not let him see me cry.

"It wasn't like he was telling the whole bar. It was just me and the twins. He seemed really beaten up about it."

"What does he have to be beaten up about? He played me. He told me what I wanted to hear, and as soon as I believed he wasn't a creep, he admitted to saying what he did to get me into bed."

My eyebrows pulled together, and my throat knotted up. "He is an ... an ... an asshole!" I spit out the first cuss word of my entire life, and that angered me even more.

Lana backed away from me like I'd slapped her in the face. "Tell me how you really feel."

"That is how I feel!"

She took the coffee from my hand before it splashed all over the bed in my rage. "It was just an expression."

I followed her into the kitchen where she emptied the paper cup and refilled it with coffee from my single cup instant brewer. When the cup was full, and she'd doctored it with creamer, she set it on the kitchen island in front of where I sat at a stool.

"If it's any conciliation, I think he hates himself as much as you hate him."

"Impossible."

"I think—"

"What?" I snapped.

"Never mind." She shook her head.

"No, I'm sorry. I'm not mad at you. You know that."

"I know. Not yet anyway." She continued after a breath for encouragement. "I think he's so bent out of shape because he knows he went too far this time and he's afraid you won't forgive him."

"Well, he's right. I won't forgive him." I took my coffee back to bed. "Why was he acting like he cares? Is he that disappointed that he won't get to conquer all the Pavers in DFW?" I threw the covers over my head. "It's embarrassing," I whined through the thick cotton. "I almost kissed him!"

"It's not embarrassing."

"Yes, it is." I threw myself onto my back and brought the covers over my head. "It's Rupert." I laughed, finally breaking into hysterics at the outrage. Just two days ago if he would have tried kissing me, I would have slapped him.

Lana laughed with me, knowing that I needed her to. "Promise to keep a secret?" Lana asked when our giggles died down.

My interest peaked enough for me to show my face from under my cotton shield.

"I mean it, you'll tell no one?"

"Pinky promise." I extended my finger.

"My first kiss—" She cleared her throat. "My first kiss was Percy," she rushed, then snagged my blanket from me and hid her beat-red face in it.

"Percy?" I laughed outright.

The white cloud nodded up and down. "You promised."

"I promised not to tell, but I didn't promise not to laugh."

With the embarrassing scores evened out, I went into detail about my night's events with Rupert. I told her about his ridiculously showy meal, and how the hostess hung on his every word. I admitted to how I had pictured what our kids would look like, even going so far as admitting I imagined myself in a big poofy white wedding dress.

I ended with, "Lana, his human alias is Rhett Butler." I felt my eyebrows pull together, and tears gathered in the corners of my eyes. I willed them to stop, but then my bottom lip started shaking.

Lana pulled my head onto her lap. "Oh, honey," she said and resumed smoothing my hair like she had first thing that morning.

"*Gone with the Wind* is my favorite ever." I sobbed. "I can never watch it again."

"I know." Lana pressed play on the remote, and we watched Felicity fall in and out and back in love with Ben and Noel until the day had gone and a new one started.

♥

Once the sun had risen, I left Lana, in her awkward angle asleep on the bed, and headed off to work. I got there early so I'd have little to no risk of running into Rupert. The day was going to be rough enough as it was, I didn't need his face to be one of the first that I saw on top of it all.

I was working on practically zero sleep, and my plate was three times as heavy as usual. I had to Kiss yesterday's couple and do damage control on Adam and Carrie since I'd left Adam's house without Kissing him. The connection between him and Carrie wasn't in motion and since more than twenty-four hours had passed since I kissed Carrie, I'd have to start over. I'd have to rush through today's assignment to allow time to go back to Denton and ignite the connection between them. I was too exhausted to even think about how I was going to make Jenny and Ivan Seal their Kiss.

I planned out my day, so I'd finish my tasks and be in bed as quickly as possible. I was tired already, and it was only seven thirty.

So far so good, I'd retrieved my assignment card (without breaking any more rules) and was waiting for Michael Cummings to show up to work so I could hurry up and move on to his Fated, Carmen Mendoza.

Apparently, there was a reason Pavers started the day at ten o'clock instead of eight like the rest of the world, no one else was at work yet. I contemplated floating through the rows of cars between Michael's home and his work but figured the chances of finding him, let alone him having his windows rolled down were slim to none. So I lingered in the front of his office and waited for him to come to me.

He was a real estate agent in Keller, and any other day, I would have loved the idea of shadowing him for hours while he sold big fancy houses to beautiful people, but my heart wasn't in it today.

With time to kill, I opened my clutch and pulled out my Fated card. I turned it over, examining the exterior carefully. My name was written perfect calligraphy—the *i* in *Darling* dotted with a heart, like it was when I signed my name.

I'd meant to put it back in the drawer it belonged in when I was at Cupid HQ earlier, but with no one to distract Daphne that early in the morning, I was forced to hang on to it. Last night, I had told Lana that I'd stolen my card, and she'd convinced me to return it without peaking.

She was right. I knew she was. The timing of when a person met their Fated was almost as important as the person.

A lot of the time, people had a creative or secondary Destiny they were to fulfill before their time came to be with their Fated. Who knew, maybe I was meant to fall in love with the wrong person before I fell in love with the right one so I could learn from my mistakes. Or maybe my Fated wasn't ready to be with me yet. It was always possible he wasn't even born yet since regular age-rules didn't apply to Pavers.

The reminder of the reasons behind the rules caused me to shake my head and slide the card back into my clutch. I was afraid if I looked at it any longer I'd throw reason to the wind and open it.

I paced in front of the real estate office until Michael Cummings climbed out of his sleek, silver sports car. I planted his Cupid Kiss square on his mouth before he even entered the building and zoomed over to Carmen Mendoza's workplace to lay one on her too. She cut hair in little salon across the street from Michael's office.

I let myself in behind her first customer, a man who didn't seem to have enough hair to spend money on a cut. Before he'd made into his chair, I walked right to Carmen and planted a quick peck on her lips and waited for the pink sparks to fly.

Nothing happened.

Setting my shoulders, I stretched my lips before puckering. Keeping my eyes open this time, I bent forward and laid a good one on her.

She swatted at her lips, shewing away the sensation of an invisible kiss, but no sparks flew.

Slack-jawed, I stepped aside to prevent getting my nose snipped off when she pulled out her scissors.

"Anything new since I saw you last?" the man asked his hairdresser.

A faint blush rose in her cheeks as she smiled. "Actually,"

she said trying to keep her voice professional. "I met someone."

The man in the seat flashed his eyes to hers in the mirror. "Oh. That's good news," he said, seeming surprised she'd shared so much. "I wasn't aware you were on the market."

She laughed, nodding as she began her work on his few hairs. "I wasn't really. I mean, I wasn't not on the market, I just wasn't actively looking. But there I was, cutting a regular's hair, when all the sudden, I looked at him, really looked at him. He caught my eyes and bam. It was like, magic."

I backed away from Carmen and her customer, so distracted by what she'd said that I'd forgotten to watch where I was going. My elbow bumped a manikin head off a shelf, causing it to clatter to the floor. The wig landed a foot away in a tangled mess.

Carmen and the man jerked their heads toward the unexplainable scene, searching for what caused the head to clamber to the floor.

Instinct kicked in. My wings buzzed, propelling me up and backward.

I had given enough Kisses to recognize the signs. Carmen had been Kissed. And not matched with her Fated.

That was the second Kiss I'd failed in three days. Third, if I counted Adam and Carrie. Panicked, I pulled out Carmen and Michael's cards, double checking the date. If they were fated for yesterday and I'd missed it because I was lounging in bed, I would have so much paperwork to fill out.

But that wasn't the case, Carmen and Michael had been Destined to be Kissed today. Not yesterday. It wasn't my fault. That fact was only slightly comforting. It didn't change the fact that my name was on their card, and I'd have some serious explaining to do. One botched Kiss was one thing, but two?

That was grounds for getting my Kiss suspended. If I didn't Kiss yesterday's couple and get to Adam and Carrie soon, I'd have three failed jobs in my name. And I wouldn't have my Kiss suspended, I'd have it revoked. And possibly my Veil, too.

Stuffing that fear away to deal with later, I pulled out the second Fated envelope from my clutch, ignoring the one that had my name on it. A quick inspection told me my day had just gotten a whole lot harder. Tyler Owens, Fated A, worked at DFW airport. I hated the airport so much that I almost always waited until the Fated was home from their shift before giving them their Kiss. But there was no time for that today.

Not wasting another second, I pushed the door open, not waiting for another customer to let me out, not caring what Carmen and her customer thought about the second phantom act. I had one last thing to do before heading to the airport.

I found Michael on the phone, a cloud of blue sparks hanging above his head, waiting to be paired with their Fated.

I'd had to do this once before. I'd been on a double that day. The first Fated I'd gone to was a fast and easy Kiss, but when I'd gone to his match, she'd locked herself in a hotel room, with no way for me to get to her. Afraid I wouldn't get to him before I missed my opportunity to get to my second couple, I took back my first Kiss so I could move onto my second pair.

This time, I wouldn't be coming back later to try again. This time, I was taking back my Kiss permanently, or until he was re-Fated.

Michael hung up his phone and walked to his filing cabinet. Without any of my usual excitement, I leaned in, a Kissed him.

The cloud above his head fizzled out.

Chapter Ten

$\mathcal{J}$ust as I'd feared, Tyler worked in the busiest terminal in the airport, meaning I'd be around a lot of people who were constantly either running late or tired of waiting around in uncomfortable chairs without their creature comforts all day. In a nutshell, travelers were grumpy.

I zipped through the airport as quickly as I could, hoping I'd selected the correct entrance, soaring over commuters' heads and dodging ceiling signs as best I could while reading my card to pinpoint Tyler's exact location. Just before smacking into a low-hanging sign, I dropped low to avoid a headache I so didn't need. In my rush to avoid the sign, I'd descended lower than I'd wanted to, resulting in a kick to a man's head.

"Watch it!" the angry businessman screamed, bending down and picking up my black pump that had fallen off in the collision. He waved it at a woman pushing a stroller.

"It's not mine," she said, maneuvering her stroller away from the man as if she feared he was going to throw the shoe at her baby.

I curled my bare toes and covered my mouth. I was a little afraid he was going to throw it at her baby too. He surely wasn't going to find the true culprit. People didn't go around assuming an invisible Cupid was to blame.

I added one more screw up to my list of reasons I was going to get my Kiss revoked.

Focusing on the task at hand, I flew higher above the mob of people to avoid another mistake and finally hovered above a crowd of people to read the airport map. According to the schedule on my assignment card, Tyler was working flight 322.

I mapped out my route and flew over the sea of people straight to baggage claim. If I'd had the time, I would scour the huge room for an employee entrance door, but that could take forever. Groaning, I assessed the most efficient way to get into the employees only area was to ride the filthy, greasy, ugly conveyor belt inside.

"Ew, ew, ew, ew, ew!" I squealed, as I floated down on top of the belt, landing on my knees. I hugged a humongous suitcase, using it to open the rubbery curtains that divided the public from the employee zones.

Just before I made it to the curtains, a man swooped in, grabbing the bag I'd been clutching. I had no choice, I released the bag. Without enough time to secure another shield, I got hit in the face by smelly, rubber curtains.

"My hair!" I should've been more worried whether or not a bystander saw the curtains part themselves than what the act did to my hair, especially when none of them could see it, but I couldn't help it.

I blew a fallen lock from my eyes and got to work. The luggage conveyer belt emptied into a warehouse-type room where dozens of employees tossed bags onto belts.

"Tyler, Tyler? Where are you?" I sang.

I pulled out my assignment card out for what seemed like the tenth time and committed Tyler's picture to memory. He was a brunette with an olive complexion. He styled his facial hair into a goatee and wore thick-rimmed glasses.

"Nope, nope and … nope." I pouted. No brown-haired dudes in glasses. I circled the room again, this time reading name tags in case he'd shaved or dyed his hair or was wearing contacts.

"Yo, Tyler!" a large man with an intimidating voice called out.

I paused, waiting for a response.

"Tyler," the man called again.

"He's over here," a guy with sandy hair from across the room shouted.

I flew closer to the voice and found Tyler playing an imaginary drum set on a suitcase.

I laughed and moved as close as I dared, wanting to plug

in my imaginary electric guitar and have a mini-jam session of my own. Before I had the chance to decide if the fun would be worth the time, the guy with the sandy hair plucked out one of his earbuds.

"What?" Tyler shoved the guy's hand away with his forearm.

"Jim's looking for you," the guy, AJ, according to his name tag, nodded in the large man's direction.

Quickly, Tyler pulled the other bud out of his ear and wrapped the set around his phone and shoved it in his pocket. He hustled over to Jim. "Looking for me?"

"Yeah, I'm looking for you. I'm always looking for you. Where were you on that unload?"

"The bath … the … the bathroom."

"Again?"

"Yes, sir. I have a small bladder."

Snickers escaped the other employees. Jim's head snapped up, and he made eye contact with the people paying more attention to Tyler than their work. Like roaches, they scurried back to their respective stations and looked busy.

"Bring a doctor's note for your, uh, bladder problems, and we'll be good. Otherwise, don't show up to work tomorrow. I'm tired of you disappearing all the time." Jim walked away without waiting for a response.

As if the weight of Tyler's reprimand rested on my shoulders, my wings slowed, and I sailed to the floor to stand next to him.

His head hung low, and he bounced his fist off his thigh.

Poor guy. I chose that moment to plant my Kiss right on his lips. The blue sparks shimmering off his mouth filled me with hope. At least he'd be in love soon. With phase one of the job done, I flew back to the conveyor belt and held on tight to a suitcase-shield to exit the warehouse.

❤

Molly Keenan, Tyler's Fated, lived with her mom and step-dad in their multi-million-dollar home. The house was breathtaking, adobe siding and Spanish tiles on the roof, not my style, but beautiful just the same.

I stared at the house, trying to decide my move. In most homes, I could find an empty room and crawl through a window or door, as undignified as it sounded. I was handy with a bobby pin.

A house of this grandeur, however, was sure to have an alarm system that would blare as soon as I started tampering with locks. It likely had security cameras that would catch a door opening and closing by itself too. No breaking and entering this time, I'd have to stake the place out.

I circled the property, hoping I'd catch a break and find Molly lounging by the pool or sitting on one of the many terraces on the property. But that would have been too convenient.

With no other option, I set up shop on one of the fancy lawn chairs by the pool, snagging a pair of forgotten sunglasses and waited for signs that someone was coming home so I could sneak in behind them.

Idle time was exactly what I didn't need. Aside from needing to be in four other places, I also didn't want to be alone with my thoughts. Or alone with the very tempting card with my name on it. A girl could only be asked to have so much willpower.

As if Lana was there watching me, my phone buzzed with a text from her. "Did you manage to sneak back into HQ and put your card back?"

"Yup," I sent. It wouldn't be a lie tomorrow.

The back door slammed shut. Molly walked out, on the phone talking quietly. Putting the sunglasses back where I'd found them, I flitted close to her, eager to get this over and done with. I needed a moment for her to get her face out of the phone so I could perform the Kiss her and go.

"My mom will never go for it," Molly explained. After a short pause, she said, "She'll know if I lie to her. I get all giggly and stutter when I lie."

The girl on the other end of the line said something indiscernible to me.

Molly grew impatient and held the phone away from her face, letting whoever the girl she was talking to ramble to no one.

I saw my opportunity to go in for the Kiss. I didn't waste a second. Gently and quickly, I pecked Molly on the lips and backed up in time to avoid getting smacked in the face with Molly's phone.

I did the most ridiculous happy dance when I saw those precious pink sparks fly from her lips. The cord that would connect her to Tyler soared through the air, on its way to find him.

"You know what?" Molly asked, eagerly. "I'll ask Chis, not Mom. He's been dying to get on my good side ever since the wedding. I won't even have to lie to him."

"Really?" blared from the other side of the phone line.

Molly shrank away from the shrill voice. "Yes, really. I'm gonna go tell him now before Mom gets home. I'll grab my clothes and makeup bag. Be at your house in twenty."

I flew away, not wanting to watch Molly take advantage of her step-dad. It could be a pure coincidence that Molly suddenly had an idea as to how the girls would get to where ever it is they were going tonight, but I was putting my money on the fact that Cupid's Kiss supplied the answer.

Chapter Eleven

*F*lying against a strong wind was like trying to run through wet sand while wearing flip-flops and carrying ten feral cats. Instead of flying high in the sky, soaring over the metroplex, I had to hug the streets, letting the buildings protect me from the wind. By the time I made it to Carrie's store, I thought my wings were going to fall right off my back. My wings sputtered and slowed, making for a hard landing on the sidewalk.

I thanked Destiny for my Veil because I knew my hair had twisted itself into something that would scare a monster, and I was still missing a shoe. I would need so much conditioner to get the tangles out.

I thought luck was on my side when I found the back door propped open like it had been the other day. But that thought was quickly squashed when learned Carrie wasn't working.

Huffing and puffing in a way that was seriously unattractive, I flew the short distance to Carrie's house. She lived with four other girls in a tiny two bedroom. All of whom were home, except the one I needed.

What now?

Giving my wings a much-needed rest, I sat on a bench in the middle of the town square and went over my options. If Adam and Carrie's Kisses weren't performed soon, Daphne would find out I was slacking. She already had a mouthful for me that morning after my day of hooky yesterday.

I supposed I could go to the school to find Carrie, but UNT was a huge campus, and it'd be next to impossible to find her without knowing which classes she took on Thursday afternoons. A glance at my cell phone told me she probably wouldn't have classes this late anyways.

Throwing my head back and wiping my hands down my face, I let out a scream that would have made dogs cry if they could hear me. Why hadn't I pecked Adam before rushing out the door to go on that stupid not-date with Rupert?

"Because part of you was too excited to get to the restaurant and part of you wasn't ready to let Adam go," I answered myself, kicking at the ground.

Shaking my head, I decided to try Adam first and hope Carrie would be home when I finished. I needed to get the Kiss over with once and for all, if for no other reason than to prove to myself that I didn't care about Adam. The fantasy I'd let myself dream up with him was just as ridiculous as the fantasy I'd dreamed up with Rupert. Both were impossible and never going to happen. I might as well come to terms with Adam the same way I had with Rupert.

Using the logic that Adam wouldn't have two days off in the work week, I put my poor, abused wings to the test, and flew to the construction site indicated in his assignment card rather than going to his home. I really needed a car.

I found Adam cutting thin pieces of wood on a table saw. He wore jeans that hugged him in all the right places, a white T-shirt, and a yellow hard hat.

Glancing around, I saw men on rooftops and second floors of houses. I plucked a hard hat for myself out of the bed of a work truck and plopped it on my head. Wind hair and hat hair. Fantastic. But it was a necessity seeing as I was in even more danger than the rest of the workers because they couldn't see me. I could just imagine being knocked over the head with a fallen two-by-four. I would lie there, passed out and invisible.

"I should get hazard pay for this," I grumbled under my breath. Zeroing in on Adam, I told myself I would Kiss him and be gone. I would not let myself get distracted by his piercing blue eyes.

Just as I was feet away, sparks flew from Adam's saw. I managed to change directions in time to avoid the flying fire from catching on my skirt.

"What?" Adam slowed his saw and pulled a bright-orange sponge from his ear.

"I asked if you wanna go out with us tonight!" A man with a painful looking sunburn screamed to Adam.

Adam slowly shook his head undecidedly, lifting his hard hat to wipe his forehead. "I don't know, man. Last time we all went out we got pretty smashed and were in a lot of pain the next morning. Saws and hammers don't help a hangover."

The sunburned man laughed. "You have to come. You haven't been out with us in a long time."

After another moment of deliberation, Adam shook his head and said, "I'll just slow y'all down. You guys go ahead." Adam plugged his ear protection back into his ear and positioned his saw.

The man waved his hands in front of Adam to get his attention. When Adam sighed and gave him his attention, the guy plastered on a guilty smile. "I kinda promised Mandy that I'd convince you to come."

"Seriously?" Adam moaned, giving up on the saw and walking toward his friend.

"Seriously. Her sister's coming in town, and you know how badly she wants to hook you guys up."

"I told you, Brian, I don't want to be hooked up. I don't even want to date. I'm not ready. Amber only died a year ago." A flash of pain streaked through Adam's face.

"You're never going to be ready until you put yourself out there. No one said you have to marry the girl, just do me a solid and meet her."

After several groans and unpleasant faces, Adam gave Brian a short nod.

"Great! Thanks, dude, you won't regret it. Mandy's sister is hot."

"Then you go for her." Adam laughed.

"I got my girl." Brian smiled. "Dan's Silverleaf at nine."

Time and place were all I'd been waiting to hear. I dropped the hard hat into the bed of the truck and headed for home. I'd have four hours to power nap, get dressed, and arrive at the rendezvous place.

My mistake had been detrimental. Adam was meant to have already met Carrie. If Adam became interested in this new girl Brian and his girl planned to set him up with, Destiny could be thrown so far out of balance that it may not ever right itself.

Chapter Twelve

$\mathcal{M}$y power nap had been nowhere near long enough, but it had done the trick. The circles under my eyes were more or less gone, and I had more energy than I had when I'd woke up that morning. After staring at the contents of my closet for too long, I decided to put on my favorite dress. It was crimson with small white polka-dots. I added a thick, white belt and pinned a white flower in the same spot Rupert had the other night.

Refusing to let thoughts of him penetrate my good mood, I selected my "girl power" playlist and cranked up the volume. I'd created the list years ago when I was still in Cupid training. Britney and Kelly brought me back to a time when I'd first started wearing makeup and picking out my own clothes. Channeling the girl I used to be, I sang along with every word as I finished my makeup routine and painted my nails.

As carefully as I could, I grabbed my matching clutch with still wet nails. Willing to risk leaving my door unlocked more than I was willing to smudge my polish trying to lock it, I flew out of my apartment and headed to Denton.

"Where are you going all dressed up?" Lana asked me as I flew past her. She was entering the Paver's city as I exited, carrying an instrument as tall as she was.

I slowed to speak with her. "Work." I knew she'd disapprove of my mission. Or worse, she'd want to come with me.

"You already went to work." She raised a brow then stopped her flight as well. The thing, a cello maybe, weighed her down, causing her to sink.

"Round two. I'm behind because we didn't work yesterday.

I'll see you tomorrow." I sped up in an attempt to avoid further investigation.

Even with her heavy load, she managed to catch up to me, grabbing my arm and forcing me to look at her. "Freya, what are you up?" Lana's squinted her eyes as if she could see my motives if she looked hard enough. "I hope you're not running off to meet Rupert."

I whirled around on her. "Come on Lana, have more faith in me than that." I sighed, knowing she wasn't going to let me go without more information. "I have to fix something. I screwed up."

She nodded, accepting my excuse. "Do you need help? I could come with you." She flew higher to offset the weight of the cello. "I'd just have to drop this off at home."

"There's no point. It's just a Cupid's Kiss thing. You'd waste your night flying to Denton and back, and you look like you have plans." I started flying backward to end the conversation.

"Be careful," she called to me, just before I escaped hearing distance. Her words were a warning for me to not get myself into trouble more than they were for my physical safety.

My phone chimed, indicating I'd received a text message, as I descended over Industrial Street. The text was from "Scum Bag." I'd changed Rupert's name in my phone to a more appropriate label with Lana during our *Felicity* marathon. I wanted to delete the message without reading it, but I wasn't strong enough.

"Can you meet me at the Parched Paver? I want to talk to you."

"I never want to see your face again." My finger hovered over the send button, but in the end, I deleted my response and put his contact on do not disturb. I had a job to do, and I wasn't going to let my boy problems get in the way.

At least two dozen people stood in a line, waiting to get through the Silverleaf's door. I was tempted to keep myself Veiled and float above the line and into the bar. I decided against it. However, I wasn't there to rush in and rush out. I was there as a patron to listen to the music, have a drink, and only get involved in Cupid business if I suspected Adam was getting too cozy with the blind date. I smiled to myself. I was a

Sprite for the night.

I landed behind between two Texas-sized trucks in a public parking lot a block away. When I was sure no one was looking, I let the Veil fall away. My back tingled as I felt my wings recede under my shoulder blades. I wasn't an expert about how the Veil worked, but anytime a Paver dropped their Veil outside of the Pavers' Cloud, their wings disappeared along with it.

After ten minutes of waiting in line, I almost regretted my choice of shoes. Only almost. They really had been a perfect match. They were black, spiked heels, with the tiniest bit of red at the tip of the peek-a-boo toe. Their cuteness didn't keep my toes from pinching or a blister on my ankle from forming, however. I wore heels almost every day, but since I was usually airborne or walking short distances in my apartment, I hadn't developed the muscles or pain tolerance or whatever it was human girls had that let them stand in heels for hours on end. I sucked up the pain, attributing it to part of the human experience I'd always wanted.

The closer I got to the front door, the louder the music thumped. For the second time in less than twenty minutes, I resisted the urge to Veil myself. I wanted to dance like no one was watching. Instead, I bobbed my head to the beat, like everyone else.

This was part of being a person in the city. I'd have to wait in line and awkwardly dance in front of complete strangers. I was really doing it, being an average person.

I finally made into the building and took in the artwork covering the bright teal walls. Each piece was unlike any I'd seen before. I wondered how many of the pieces Lana had a hand in creating.

"Hello," I said to a long-haired guy with a beard about my apparent age sitting on a stool, guarding the entryway.

"ID?"

"Oh, yeah." I giggled and pulled out my driver's license with my alias, Julie Capulet. The card said twenty-one. Perks of getting your government paperwork from a cloud in the sky.

"Cover is fifteen."

I furrowed my brow. Cover? What is cover?

"Dollars." He reassessed my ID with furrowed brows before handing it back. "Fifteen dollars to get in tonight."

"Oh, right." I giggled again, handing him a twenty.

He handed me my change and stamped my hand with a metallic silver leaf.

Deciding it was the most natural thing to do, I headed to the bar to order a drink, all the while looking through the crowd for Adam. The assortment of people was among the most diverse I'd ever seen in one place. Groups of college kids with trendy clothing were scattered about middle-aged hippies, cowboys, and grannies, all of them dancing in whatever way suited them.

I smoothed my skirts self-consciously. It seemed that anyone with any style fit in, but none of them were dressed as formally as I was. Lana and her layers and dreadlocks would have blended into the scene a lot easier.

Just as I was about to abort my human-experience mission and Veil myself, a squad of girls in tight, showy dresses walked by with linked arms. Their clubbing-chic style was much different than mine but no less formal. I didn't stick out as badly as I'd thought.

With growing confidence, I loosened my head-bob into a more relaxed shoulder grove, appreciating the music as I closed the distance to the bar.

"What can I get you, doll?" A tall bartender with a bandana around his neck asked me.

I opened my mouth to order a Cosmo but changed my mind. It was an opportunity to exercise my option to choose. This bartender had no idea who I was. The feeling was glorious. "Surprise me," I shouted above the music.

He shrugged and turned away to make my surprise. He returned a moment later and handed me a tall glass, filled to the brim with dark brown liquid and an inch of white foam. I stared at as if it were a bug. I'd never liked beer, and in the small experience that I had with it, I'd found that the darker the beer, the worse it tasted.

I paid the man anyway. And brought it to my lips, resisting the urge to plug my nose. The beer left a terrible taste in my mouth, and I puckered to hold in a burp.

"Not a beer-girl?" A smooth, deep voice said from my right side.

Startled, I blew a surprised breath into the beer. Foam sloshed from the lip of the glass, and I set it down to avoid spilling it all over myself.

The voice belonged to Adam. His strong, sleeved arm brushed against my bare own as he leaned against the bar.

I swallowed my surprise and shined my brightest smile at him. "Not at all," I admitted. "But it's my fault, I shouldn't have let the bartender have free reign over my beverage choice."

"What can I get you?" The bandana-wearing bartender asked Adam.

Adam smirked at me before ordering his drink. "A Dirty Shirley."

The bartender raised a single brow. "Dirty Shirley?"

"Yup." Adam smiled.

He shook his head but turned to make the drink. I watched as he flipped a bottle of vodka upside down in a tall glass with ice. He added a clear liquid from his soda gun and dripped a pink, thick syrup into it. It looked a lot tastier than my beer.

Topping it off with a cherry, the bartender set the glass in front of Adam. "One Dirty Shirley."

"Keep the change," Adam said, shoving cash into the bartender's hand.

"Lucky for you, I am a beer guy." He took the beer off the bar-top and replaced it with the cocktail. He clinked the beer on my new glass and winked. "Cheers," he said and took a swig of the dark-brown liquid.

I put the straw in my mouth and sipped on my new drink. "This is great."

"Thought you might like that one. I bartended while I was in college. You look like a pink-drink type, not a stout-beer drinker. But you're missing out. This beer is mmm-mmm good." As if to prove it, Adam swallowed another mouthful.

I played with the straw between my teeth and stared at him, smiling stupidly.

He wore a bright-blue, button-up shirt with little pearls for buttons tucked into form-fitting jeans. His hair, though styled, went every which way on his head like it was rebelling against the hair-gel.

This was what a man looks like. I compared his appearance to Rupert's over-styled hair and designer clothes.

Rupert wore too much cologne, but the left-over scent that stayed on my clothes after he touched me was just right.

I love it.

Loved it.

I wouldn't think about the way he smelled anymore.

I leaned in a little closer to Adam to compare his scent to Rupert's. Adam smelled the same way he had the other day, like men's body wash. It was intoxicating.

"Well, you pegged me right. This drink is good."

"It's nothing fancy, Sprite, vodka, and grenadine."

"Oh, I get it." I laughed. "A spiked Shirley Temple."

"Exactly."

"There you are." Adam's friend, Brian, busted our bubble.

"Hey, Brian. Hey, Mandy." Adam nodded a hello.

"This is Andrea. Andie, this is Brian." Mandy, a cute brunette with wild, curly hair, screamed over the music, gesturing to a drop-dead gorgeous blonde with legs that went forever in one direction, and a chest that went forever in another.

This was going to be harder than I thought.

"Ouch. Andie and Mandy? Your parents have a twisted sense of humor," Adam joked.

"We're step-sisters," Andie shot back, not amused. "I drink grey goose martinis," she said to Adam as if he was her bartender. "Dry. With a twist. Not olives," she added as an afterthought.

Adam's eyebrows sky-rocketed to his hairline.

"Andie," Mandy chastised under her breath.

"What? He's standing in front of the bar, and he's supposed to be my date, so he's going to order it anyway," she said, snapping a selfie.

Adam turned toward the bar, making eye contact with me. His expression was both amused and irritated.

A tall brunette with tattoos covering every visible part of her arms and chest stood ready to take his order. "What can I get for you, boss?"

"A wet grey goose martini with a twist, please," Adam said.

"No olives," Andie called, finishing her command with an, "ugh."

"And two Shiners," Brian added, throwing money on the bar, paying for all three drinks.

"It's really crowded in here," Andie said, her voice coming out in a whine. She turned on her heal and headed toward the large patio behind the bar.

"But this is where the music is," Brian said, pointing to the band.

She continued walking.

"I guess we're going outside." Adam clanked his glass against mine. "Thanks for the beer."

"Thanks for the Dirty Shirley."

In a matter of seconds, I was squeezed out of my spot at the bar by thirsty customers trying to order drinks and found myself surrounded by a dozen people having their own screaming conversations over my head. I was too short to see the band from the back, and I wasn't brave enough to elbow my way from the front. So I casually made my way to the patio, needing to keep an eye on Adam and Andie. Not that I foresaw them hitting it off.

The patio was larger than I'd anticipated, sprawling out behind the business next door. Another bar, with its own bartender, served drinks to almost as many people as inside. Though there was a stage, no one was performing, so groups of people sat on its edge, drinking and laughing. Every table and chair was occupied.

I loomed close to a group of people standing at the edge of the bar so I could watch Adam and Andie without being obvious.

Brian and Mandy carried on a conversation amongst themselves, trying to include their hostages, but neither Andie nor Adam were being very cooperative.

I felt giddy about that. I told myself was happy because, as it turned out, I hadn't caused as much harm by not completing the Cupid's Kisses as I'd thought I had. But in truth, I was happy Adam wasn't impressed with the snotty girl. I was glad he wasn't happy with any girl.

I felt a tingle on my arm where Adam's sleeve had brushed

against me earlier, and I touched the spot, willing the feeling to stay.

I only snapped back to the present because Andie's martini glass tipped itself over. The liquid inside rained onto her white blouse. I caught a laugh in my mouth before it escaped.

"Are you serious?" Andie yelled. She hopelessly wiped at the mess on her shirt with her hands, but her blouse was so thin it had already absorbed the moisture, and the stain spread wider on her chest. "Napkins," she demanded of anyone who was listening.

No one rushed to grab her any.

"Anyone?"

"Oh, you're asking for napkins?" Adam asked, pretending to have just realized her meaning.

"Duh."

Mandy rushed past me to the bar. She grabbed a handful, and returned to the table, dabbing at Andie's shirt with them.

Andie snatched the wet clump out of Mandy's hand and took over. "You're making it worse." Without excusing herself, Andie stomped away from the table.

Brian made eye contact with Adam and shook his head in apology.

Adam shrugged and gulped a mouthful of beer.

Andie had almost made her way to where I stood when she tripped over her own feet. She braced herself on my arm, righted herself, and headed to the bathroom without so much as an apologetic glance my way.

The interaction, if you could call it that, between Andie and me brought Adam's attention my way. He shook his head and gave me the same apologetic look Brian had given him.

I lifted a shoulder and smiled.

We watched each other drink our drinks and smiled back and forth until my whole body was covered in goose bumps.

A small, pink ball landed in Adam's beer, averting his attention from me. Beer splashed out of his cup, landing on his shirt and face. Instead of demanding napkins or throwing a tantrum, he laughed and licked at the liquid that had splashed his lips.

"Who's playing beer pong?" Brian asked.

They looked around, trying to find the source. Without an obvious one, Adam shrugged it off, pulled the ball from his glass, and took another drink. He noticed me still watching him when he pulled the glass from his face.

Heat ran over my cheeks, and I looked away.

A moment later, someone tapped me on the shoulder.

Letting myself hope it was Adam, I turned slowly with a smile. He was still with his group, too far away to have been the tapper, but he was still looking at me and returned my smile. The heat in my cheeks spread through my body, filling every inch of me.

We stayed like that, locked in eye contact until a very unwelcome Andie returned from the bathroom. He may have stopped looking at me, but I couldn't stop watching him. Every move he made was hypnotic. The way he talked with his hands, the way his shirt stretched over his chest when he leaned back, even the way he rubbed his hand over the stubble on his cheek was captivating. I could watch him for hours.

The ball he'd discarded moments ago hit me in the leg, but I hadn't seen who'd thrown it. I bent over to retrieve it from between several pairs of feet sitting at the outdoor bar. Rolling it around in my hand, I realized that the ball was familiar.

I stood straight and searched the crowd for a specific set of twins. The left side of my dress pitched up, then the right. I looked from one side to the other, but I didn't see anyone there.

The ball disappeared from my hand.

"Percy and Penny," I groaned.

The back of my skirt flew up.

I whirled around, trying to spot them even though I knew it was hopeless.

My phone chimed in my purse, followed by a second chime.

The first text was from Percy, "Happy to see us?"

The second is from Penny, "Oh wait you can't! LOL."

"What are y'all doing here?" I responded to both of them in the group message.

"Cleaning up your mess," Percy responded.

"My mess? Did Sprites HQ send you?"

"Yes, little missy, they did," Penny answered.

"They know you didn't complete your assignment," Percy texted.

"And we have to make sure he doesn't fall in love with anyone else in the process," Penny explained.

In a separate, private message Penny sent me another text. "Don't worry, Cupid HQ isn't involved yet."

I sighed in relief. "You guys can go home. I'm taking care of it," I sent it to both of them.

My phone chimed two more times, but I ignored it because Adam had walked over and was standing next to me. "I have to get another martini for my date." His eyes danced with laughter.

"Is that your girlfriend?" I played dumb.

"Ha. Hardly." Adam laughed. "She's my buddy's girl's step-sister. They've been trying to get us to go out for almost six months. I now understand how a pretty girl like her has managed to stay single for so long."

"It's a mystery," I agreed.

"Can I get a Grey Goose martini, wet with a twist, a tall Guinness, and a Dirty Shirley?" Adam asked the bartender, a small-framed man with a T-shirt and tie.

"You don't have to do that," I said and reached for my money.

"Nah, but I want to."

I smiled. "Guinness? Is that the beer I inadvertently ordered for you earlier?"

"Yup. I don't know what that bartender was thinking giving it to you."

"I'm sure it's a good beer if you aren't me."

"Are you here by yourself?" Adam looked around, pretending he hadn't seen me by alone earlier.

"Well, kinda," I told him as much of the truth as I could. "My friends are here somewhere. I just haven't seen them yet."

My phone continued chiming.

"This place is packed. I can see why. It's great. It's my first time here, you?"

"Yep, my first time, too."

"I wish I could be in there listening to the music." Adam nodded toward the indoor stage.

"I tried, but I got swallowed up by the crowd. I can hear it though. It's nice." I tapped my foot to the beat.

"Here you go." The bartender sat three drinks in front of Adam.

My phone chimed again, and I silenced it.

"That's probably your friends. I have to get back to my date anyway." He said "date" like it hurt him.

"Have fun." I checked my phone after watching him walk away.

"Someone get Freya a drool bucket," was the first text from Percy in the group message,

"You're staring …" Penny had added.

"You better watch out," Percy's last text said in the group message.

"Watch out?" I said aloud.

"He can't fall in love with *anyone*," Penny answered in the group message. Privately she added, "Don't fall for him, girl. That will be a lot bigger mess for us to clean up, and you won't like what we'll have to do."

"Secrets, secrets are no fun, unless they are for me!" Percy texted us.

"Don't worry about me," I told them both. "I'm just working."

My phone went blissfully silent. I hadn't believed they'd really left, but I was hoping they'd at least back off the ball throwing and skirt pulling. It didn't take long for my eyes to wander back to Adam. I couldn't help myself, he was so handsome.

Brian had him locked in a conversation, but every so often his eyes slid back to mine.

Penny arrived at my side, unVeiled, jarring my attention away from Adam. "Let's go home. He's not gonna fall in love with that priss." When I opened my mouth to argue, she added, "Freya, please."

Without a viable excuse, I nodded in agreement, giving Adam a longing look as I walked toward the patio's back door with Penny and an invisible Percy at my side.

As soon as the gate closed behind us, Percy's Veil enveloped Penny and me. We were invisible to everyone but each other as we rose in flight toward home.

I heard the gate swing open and shut again, looking back, I found Adam standing alone, looking for me.

Chapter Thirteen

"Freya, no!" Percy and Penny called at the same time. Penny grabbed my arm, preventing me from swooping down and landing on the ground.

I wanted to run to Adam. I imagined how the night could have ended if I was a girl leaving the bar, walking to her car, instead of an invisible Cupid flying off to a cloud in the sky.

In my mind's eye, he catches up to me in time. His hand falls on my arm, and I spin toward him. His crazy-blue eyes roam over my face, taking in every feature. I do the same, eating up every inch of his face with my eyes. "You can't go yet," he says. "Not without a goodnight kiss." He scoops me into his big strong, arms and dips me, kissing me long and sweet.

Percy grabbed my other arm, helping Penny. I'd apparently dragged her down in my desperation to get to Adam. Together, the twins pulled me higher and higher into the air until I could no longer see Adam walking through the parking lot, searching for me.

Once he was no longer in sight, I stopped fighting them. I'd still wanted to go to him, but the distance had helped clear my head.

"I can stay with you tonight," Penny said when we reached my front door. They'd flown me all the way home like a hostage, fearful I'd gone mad and couldn't be trusted not to turn around and find Adam.

"No, we can't," Percy said, looking at Penny like she'd left her mind at the bar. With my heart.

"I said that I could stay with her. I didn't say anything

about you." Penny's hand landed on her hip.

"Neither of you has to stay with me. I won't do anything rash." I pulled my arm out of Penny's grip, rubbing at the spot she'd been holding. It wasn't sore, but I was angry that her hand had been where Adam's was. He wasn't the last person who'd touched it anymore.

Penny's voice was void of the sing-song rhythm she used when she was doing a bit with Percy. "I know you aren't going to do anything. But I thought you might want a friend. You've had a rough week. First with Rupert, now that guy down there. I know I wouldn't want to be alone."

I could see in her eyes that she was sincere. She and Percy seemed to never have a care in the world, but at that moment, I saw Penny as an individual, not one of the twins.

"You don't have to stay," I said, disarming my tone. "But if you wanted to come in for a while, I suppose that'd be nice." Then after a moment of thought, I looked at Percy. "You too."

"Oh, no." Penny shook her head. "It's a girls' night. No boys allowed." Penny's lips formed into a straight, unyielding line.

"What am I supposed to do?" Percy complained.

"Go to the Parched Paver and see if you can make some guy friends. You need boy time as much as us girls need our time together. Alone," she added when Percy opened his mouth to argue.

Rejected, Percy flitted away, looking over his shoulder at Penny like he couldn't believe she wasn't following him.

The door slammed behind him, and Penny convulsed in full body shakes—arms pumping and legs kicking. She let a visible shiver run through her whole body, and she hung her head back. "Ahhhh."

"What was that?" I laughed.

She smiled a bit guiltily at me. "I know I blamed your bad week on the girls' night. And it is true, I do want to be here for you. But you have no idea how badly I want a night as a girl, not an annoying Sprite-twin."

"I bet," I said, climbing out of my painful heels and setting my clutch down on the entryway table. "I don't know what I'd do if I never had a second to myself. All three of my sisters live in a huge apartment on the top floor, but as soon as I saved enough money, I got my own place. I don't know how y'all do it."

"Your sisters don't seem all that bad. At least they're girls. Percy is a slob, and he can't be serious for a second."

"Girls are catty. And they go into each other's closets and re-categorize it to be mean."

"That sounds a little personal," Penny said, walking into my apartment and looking around for the first time.

I'd known her as long as I could remember, even longer than Lana, but she'd never been in my apartment before. She did need this girl's night.

"Oh my gosh, I love that!" Penny pointed over my head. "Our place is so boring. We couldn't agree on colors or a style, so we left it the way it came."

There was nothing 'love' worthy that I could remember in the direction she was looking. I turned to see what had caught her attention.

Above my small dining room table, hung the picture frame I'd bought at Carrie's shop. Inside of it, was the black and white classic picture of a sailor kissing a nurse at the end of World War II. Beneath the frame, resting on the table, was an enormous bouquet of red roses and baby's breath. An envelope sat propped against the white jeweled vase.

"What in the world?" I flew closer to the table to get a better look.

Written in small, tight print, "Juliet" was on the front.

Recognizing the handwriting even before I made the connection to the play on my alias, I knew Rupert had been the one who'd left the arrangement for me. Tears stung at my eyes, and my hand shook as I reached for the letter.

"Is that a love note? You are so lucky. I've never gotten a love note. Or flowers. Or any gift from a guy at all. Not unless you count Percy, and I don't." Penny gushed on about how jealous she was of me, but I tuned her out.

The room scaled down to me and the note.

Half of me couldn't wait to open it. The other half wanted to rip it up and throw it away unread. I had the same feeling about my assignment card which was still in my blue clutch.

I looked toward it on the entry-way table then looked back to the envelope in my hand. Giving in to the less detrimental card, I tugged the envelope from Rupert open.

♥

Freya,

I was having a great time with you. I don't know why I went and ruined it. When you said you didn't know who I was, I got mad. Because I know everything about you.

I know what movies you like. I know what makes you laugh. I know that you want to live your life down there with the real people, just like I do. I know that you love big, romantic gestures. I know that you hate cream cheese. I know that your favorite season is spring. I know that when you're mad, you hold your breath. I know that you dress to match your mood. I know that your nostrils flare when you're trying not to laugh at my bad lines. I know that your middle name is Marie. I know that your hair naturally parts to the right, but you style it to the left to show off your mole. I know that you walk every chance you get. I know that you listen to Britney Spears to cheer you up. I know you've never been swimming. I know that you are the most beautiful woman I've ever seen.

I know that I went too far this time and I don't think you can forgive me. And that scares the hell out of me.

I am so sorry,

Rhett

♥

I read the note over and over until I could hear Rupert's voice saying the words. And then I read it until I recalled the moment he'd learned each of those things about me. There had never been a twenty-questions type conversation between us. They were tidbits and factoids he'd learned about me over the years we'd known each other. He'd learned of my hatred for cream cheese when we were eight or nine, and our teacher had brought bagels to school. I didn't know how learned my middle name. I'd guarded that fact my whole life.

"Who's it from? What does it say?" Penny asked when I looked up through misty eyes.

"Rupert." My voice was barely audible.

I handed her the note, remembering he'd texted me earlier. I rushed to my clutch, pulling my phone from it and changed his contact back to normal.

Six chimes dinged in rapid succession. I read through the messages, starting with the one I'd already read.

"Can you meet me at the Parched Paver? I want to talk to you."

"Please Freya, I have to apologize."

"I'm a total jerk, and I know it."

"I didn't mean to hurt you."

"Please answer me."

"I'm sorry. Do you believe me?"

"I'm coming over."

By the time I'd finished reading the texts, Penny had finished reading the letter. "Go to him."

"I can't," I whispered.

"Why not?"

"It's just another attempt to get under my skin," I said. Letting myself hope was too much.

"I don't think so." Penny shook her head. "A guy like Rupert doesn't write stuff like this every day. And not to just anyone."

I looked into her eyes, wide and trusting. I wanted to believe her, but I didn't know if I could. Had she ever had a guy in her life at all? Was she even more naïve than me?

"I'll go to him, but not tonight. Tonight is girls' night. Remember?" I said, wiping tears from my cheeks.

Penny smiled and jumped up and down, clapping. "What does 'a girls' night' actually mean?"

Chapter Fourteen

"I don't think this is what I had in mind," Penny said an hour later. She was wearing my pink, fluffy robe, her hair was in sponge curlers, her freshly painted purple toes were separated by foam dividers, and her face was covered in a green mask. Even through the thick coat of goo, I could see she was making a face.

"This is a girls' night, and that's what you wanted." I laughed.

"I can't picture Lana with this stuff all over her face," she whined.

"That's because Lana has never let me do it," I admitted, laughing harder.

She tossed a throw pillow at my own masked face and screamed in delight. "I can't believe you!"

I caught the pillow before it hit me. "Wanna take a picture? Percy is never going to believe me."

"Don't you dare." Penny's eyes widened as she ran into my bathroom to wash off the evidence.

"It's supposed to be on until it dries."

Penny put her hands on her hips and frowned. "No pictures!"

"No pictures."

"So, since we're having a girls' night, we might as well do it right, right?" Penny pulled a loose thread on my robe she was wearing.

"What does that mean?"

She hesitated and lowered her gaze. "Do you think I could try on a dress?"

My eyes widened, and I sprang to my closet. Penny was at least three sizes smaller than me so I wouldn't have a wide selection for her to choose from. In the very back, I found a black, slim-fitting dress from when I was only fourteen or fifteen. Even if it matched my new style, I'd never be able to fit in it again. "Have this one." I shoved the dress at her.

"I don't need to have it. I just wanna see what I look like in one."

"Every girl needs a little black dress."

"Where would I even wear it?"

"Anywhere. Everywhere. I wear dresses every day."

"That's you. Not me."

"Come on, try it on. You can wear it with some funky tights and dress it down or throw on some sling-backs and make the boys drool over you."

"No guy will ever drool over me."

I shoved the dress toward her. "Wash your mask off. I'm going to prove you wrong."

With a freshly cleaned face, Penny sat on my toilet.

My makeup bag and I had our way with her face.

She wore bold eyeshadow every day, playing to her light and fun side. That style showed off her personality, yes, but I wanted to show her how much of a drop-dead looker she was. She had enormous blue eyes and a petite mouth with a natural pout encompassed in a round face. Her skin was so flawless, she didn't need foundation, which was a good thing because she was several shades paler than me. But I added bronzer to accentuate her cheekbones and smoothed it over her lids for shine. Her eyes were so expressive, I could have left her like that, but I added a smoky liner for definition.

"I can't believe you're putting makeup on me at eleven at night."

"It's Friday. The night is young. Stop moving, I can't put mascara on you if your eyes are rolling around."

"It's not like anyone but you will see it anyway."

I smiled. "Well, we could go to the Parched Paver and show you off." I wanted Penny to see how much attention she'd get from all the guys, but I also know that there is a good chance that Rupert will be there. Waiting to see if I came to find him, maybe?

"You should go no matter what," she said. "I'll go with you, but I'm not wearing that dress." She pointed to the dress still on its hanger hanging on my closet door.

"We'll see."

After Penny's makeup was flawless and I'd pulled the sponge rollers out of her short hair, I instructed her to put on the dress while I re-made my own face. As I painted on my red lips, I caught sight of Penny in the mirror. "Wow!"

The dress fit her perfectly. Her uber-slim frame was precisely the type of body the dress was designed for, clinging to every curve, making them pop. "You look beautiful."

"I feel like a little girl playing dress-up." She looked down at herself.

"Close your eyes. But don't squint, you'll mess up your make up." I dragged her to my full-length mirror at my front door. "Look at you."

Penny opened her eyes one at a time, then her mouth dropped open. "That's me?"

"That's you!"

Seeing herself in the mirror was the convincing Penny needed. "What shoes do I wear with this?"

"What size are you?"

"Eight."

"Perfect." I brought her into my closet and opened the door. "Take your pick. That's the beauty of black, any shoes match."

Penny opened her eyes even wider at the site of my dozens of shoes laying neatly in a row. "Have enough shoes?"

"No," I told her, laughing. "There's a perfect pair for every dress. I have three dresses I haven't worn because I don't have the right shoes."

"Why'd I ask?"

Penny chose a pair of neon-green pumps. They wouldn't have been my first choice for that dress, but they were perfect for her—fun, loud, and a bit crazy.

I guided her to the closet by the front door. It had been intended to be used as a coat closet but was where I stored my purses. I riffled through the hangers of handbags and the shelves of clutches until I found what I was looking for.

"Have enough purses?"

"Have to have a purse for every pair of shoes."

"Of course you do." But her sass was cut off when I showed her the purse I was after—black with a neon-green galaxy sparking on the flap. "Cool!"

I smiled. "Keep it, I've never used it. Found it at a thrift store in Irving, but never found the dress that goes with it."

With Penny's outfit complete, we set off to the Parched Paver, for her to turn as many heads as possible.

And for me to turn *one*.

Chapter Fifteen

"Cosmo?" Dave asked as I walked in, already reaching for my usual glass.

"Actually no." I smiled. "I want a Dirty Shirley."

"A dirty what?" Lana asked, surprised.

"A Dirty Shirley," I said proudly.

"That's what the cute guy at the bar ordered for her." Penny pulled herself into the chair between Lana and me.

"Penny?" Lana looked at Penny for a second time. "I didn't even recognize you."

Penny twirled around in her chair. "I let Freya dress me like a doll to cheer her up. She's all sad that Percy and I wouldn't let her stay and flirt with her assignment."

I winced, peering at Lana through one eye.

Lana's eyes narrowed on me. "That's what you were doing? I warned you about that."

"I wouldn't have done anything stupid," I lied, remembering how close I'd been to rushing back to Adam.

Adam. I remembered the pull I had toward him perfectly, but more like how you remember a dream perfectly. I didn't know if it was the reality of being pulled away from him or finding Rupert's note that had done it, but the feelings I had for him hours ago seemed like I hadn't felt them in years.

Lana looked at me, suspicious. "You let her come with you and not me?" Hurt wasn't an expression I saw on Lana's face often, but I'd suspected the raised brows and tucked lips were a sign I'd wounded her. Penny had always been a part of our gang, sure, but more like a bonus expansion pack. Lana and I had always been the base of our clique.

"Percy and I caught her," Penny said, likely picking up on the tension between Lana and me. "We were sent to keep the guy from falling in love with the wrong person because somebody didn't intact Cupid's Kiss on time." She pointed to me from behind a cupped hand. "We didn't know Freya was the one we were supposed to keep him from."

Jealousy forgotten, Lana dropped her jaw. "You were with him two days ago. Why didn't you do it? I knew something wasn't right with you."

"What are you, my mom?" I asked, only half kidding.

"No. I know you."

Her wording, "I know you," reminded me of why I came out in the first place—Rupert. I looked up to find him but found Dave in my line of vision instead.

"Here's your Dirty Shirley. You could have told me it's a Shirley Temple with vodka. I had to look it up." He laughed, leaning into Lana. "Another beer?"

She shook her head at Dave then looked back at me. "Is Adam the cute guy at the bar?"

"Penny?" Dave asked, astonished. "Who knew you were a girl?"

"Um, everybody?" Penny wrinkled her nose. She and Dave weren't the best of friends. There were only so many broken glasses a guy could put up with before he yelled at the thrower of the ball.

"Isn't she gorgeous?" I asked him. "I put a little makeup on her, but mostly I highlighted what was already there."

"Don't avoid the question," Lana said, grabbing my attention.

I didn't answer her and took a big drink from my glass instead. "It doesn't matter. I was just mad at Rupert and was looking to have a little fun."

"Was? As in not anymore?" Lana's eyes brightened. "What happened? Did you finally let him apologize?"

I wagged my head from side to side. "No, but he did anyway. While I was gone, he kinda let himself into my apartment and left me flowers and a picture—and this note." I pulled the envelope from my clutch and handed it to her for her to read. She snatched it from me.

"You should see the flowers; they are so gorgeous," Penny gushed. "How did he get in your apartment anyway? Does he have a key?"

"I didn't lock it."

"Still, he let himself in?"

I shrugged. I probably should have been bothered by that, but I wasn't.

I watched Lana's face as she read, trying to pinpoint what part she was on based on her expression. Somewhere toward the end, her face crumpled into the "oh my gosh, how sweet" face people reserved for puppies and proposals.

"I think I might believe him," I said quietly once Lana looked up from the note.

Penny clapped and shrieked happily.

"You should believe him." Lana lowered her voice. "He's been here all night, hoping you'd come here before you went home. He's really down, Freya. He sat here with me all night telling me how much he messed up and how thinks you could be the one."

"The One? Did he say that?"

Lana nodded. "He did."

Sucking in a breath, I sat down my glass to search the room for him again.

"Who's your friend?" A male voice asked me. It belonged to Jared, an Elve. He elbowed me, suggesting I should introduce him to my new, pretty friend.

"It's me!" Penny giggled.

"Penny?" Jared's eyebrows shot up. "Who would have known you are so beautiful without your brother hogging all of the attention?"

"Oh hush." Penny swatted the attention away flirtatiously.

Jared flew to my other side so he could carry on a conversation with Penny more intimately.

I turned my attention back to Lana. "If he's been here all night, where is he now?" I hoped he hadn't given up on me and gone home for the night.

"I don't know. He was just here." Lana looked around the room. Her face took on an oh-crap look, and I followed her gaze to the back of the bar. Jacqueline was pressed against the wall by a guy kissing her neck—a tall brunette guy, wearing a polo shirt.

Before I was aware I'd left my seat, I'd flown over to Rupert and tapped him on the shoulder. As soon as he'd released Jacqueline's neck from his lips and his face turned to find out who is trying to get his attention, I slapped him as hard as I could.

Aggression flashed through his face before he saw I was the one who'd hit him. Then his aggression crumpled into pain. "Freya," he said quietly.

"Don't." His voice saying my name was too much. "Don't talk to me ever again."

I had the small satisfaction of watching Jacqueline give him a slap of her own before I turned around and left him.

"Freya, please, let me explain." He flew in front of me, preventing me from walking any further.

"Explain? There is nothing to explain. You can't go two days without making out with some girl." I shoved my hand in Jacqueline's direction. Natasha was wiping tears from her friend's eyes.

He followed behind me, talking. "As soon as I saw you, I came rushing to apologize. You have to believe me. But then I overheard you talking about that guy. The one from the bar. And I got so mad."

I whirled on him. "If you would have eavesdropped for another second, you would have heard me bragging to Lana about the flowers you left and that stupid note that I fell for." I choked back tears. "I came here for you. To tell you that I forgave you." I laughed at my own stupidity. "I can't believe how much of an idiot I am. Shame on you if you fool me once, shame on me if you fool me twice, right?" I shoved past him, hard.

"Freya, please," he begged, flying in front of me again.

"Never say my name again." I clutched at my heart.

His face contorted in pain. "Freya,"

I flinched.

"Listen to me, please." His eyes flew about my face, searching. Searching for what? "I think, think I'm in love with you, Freya." He put his hand on the side of my face, forcing me to hear his words.

I tightened my mouth, trying to think of the right words to say to tell him how cruel his words were. How much they hurt me. How he'd ruined the first time I'd ever hear those words said to me. And how ten minutes ago, those were the exact words I'd wanted to hear. I closed my eyes and let the tears spill over silently.

"I hate you." The words come out in a grumble, my throat catching them, but I knew he heard me.

All the hope died in his eyes, and he moved aside so I could leave.

Chapter Sixteen

$\mathscr{I}$ couldn't think of anything I'd rather do less than go to a wedding, but I'd committed to go to Clint and Marjorie's wedding weeks ago. They'd been one of my assignments last year. I had been feeling especially romantic at the time, so I'd held off on performing the Kiss and took the time to introduce them the old-fashioned way. I performed the Kiss long after I'd made friends with them individually and played matchmaker. And because they knew that without me there would be no them, they asked me to tell the story of their meeting at the reception.

I had been so excited to hear they were finally tying the knot and so touched that they'd asked me to be a part of their special day that I'd accepted their invitation eagerly.

Thinking about how delighted I was for them, I shoved my heartbreak down deep and pulled myself out of the bed I'd spent the last fifteen hours in and climbed into the shower like a zombie.

I didn't let myself cry, knowing that once I started, I wouldn't stop. Instead, I pulled together the story in my head of their meeting to create a speech. I dressed, did my hair, and applied my make up on auto-pilot until the speech was perfect.

A few times, my mind wandered to the moment when Rupert told me that he was in love with me, and I pretended that it didn't happen, willing myself to feel nothing. Even when the defeated look on Rupert's face when I'd told him I hated him crawled into my head, I refused to confront the feelings building inside of me.

♥

I felt more like myself as soon as I saw Marjorie walk through the church's doors. She was stunning. Her dress was absolutely to die for. Long and elegant, the white fabric hugged her figure perfectly, only fanning out at her feet. She'd opted for a birdcage, instead of a classic Veil, and it was without a doubt the right call. Her red lips were the only pop of color on her entire ensemble, matching the red roses in her bouquet exactly. I wondered if she'd picked the shade of lipstick to match the flowers or the flowers to match her lipstick. Either way, the end result was fantastic.

It wasn't until I soaked in every ounce of her beauty that I even noticed the man with salt and pepper hair walking her down the aisle, tears welling up in his eyes as he passed his daughter's hand into Clint's eager one.

My own tears were dripping like a faucet down my face, and I suppressed gargled sobs into my handkerchief. I wasn't used to appearing at weddings unVeiled. I'd gone to almost every one of my assignments' celebrations, but never as a guest, just a loud blubbering fly on the wall.

The man next to me, middle-aged and a tad creepy, handed me a fresh hanky when mine became saturated with tears.

"Thank you," I whispered.

"I have a shoulder to cry on if you need it." He winked.

I took a step away from him, flashing a "thanks but no thanks" grin.

I'd almost pulled myself together when it came time for the happy couple to exchange vows. But the tears started all over when Clint recited an adapted version of Ed Sheeran's song *Thinking Out Loud,* phrasing it like a question and a promise. "When your legs don't work like they used to before, and I can't sweep you off of your feet, will your mouth still remember the taste of my love? Will your eyes still smile from your cheeks? I promise that Darling I, will, be lovin' you past seventy."

I started using the underside of my dress to wipe away gallons of salt water falling from my eyes when Marjorie responded to Clint's vows with her own spoken version of Adele's *Make You Feel My Love.*

"When the rain is blowing in your face, and the whole world is on your case I will offer you a warm embrace to make you feel my love. I'll make you happy, make your dreams come true. There's nothing that I wouldn't do. I'll go to the ends of the Earth for you to make you feel my love."

Their unique promise to each other embodied everything I knew that love could be. I knew it was everything that it would be for me one day. I couldn't believe I'd let Rupert make me second guess how wonderful true love was.

These two, Marjorie and Clint, had found their epic love, and I knew I would too. I had a Fated card—one with my name on it—promising that I had an epic love just as Marjorie did, just as Clint did. One day, I'd be the one standing up there in the white gown looking in my Fated's eyes, promising to love him forever and always.

My thigh burned. Inside of the handbag resting on my lap was the card that held the name of my Fated. The temptation to open it and read the name, just to know who he was overcame me.

I was done waiting around and getting my heart annihilated in the process.

I promised to let myself peak as soon as I'd given my speech. As soon as my duty was done, I'd know, for once and for all, who I was meant to be with and I could forget that Rupert existed.

I stood and applauded with the congregation, celebrating Marjorie and Clint's first kiss as man and wife just as much I was celebrating my newly found peace.

♥

I gave my speech before the maid of honor and the best man toasted the bride and groom, and flawlessly if I said so myself. I told the newlyweds' loved ones how I'd met Marjorie at a yoga class and approached her afterward because I couldn't help but notice that she'd cried all the way through the corpse pose at the end of the session. We'd gone out for coffee, and she told me all about the string of losers she'd been dating. She explained how that when she'd been lying there, on her yoga mat, in the corpse pose, she'd given into a moment of self-pity at the thought of dying alone.

Later that day, I'd met Clint at a bookstore, where he'd mistaken me for an employee and sought me out to help him find a self-help book about how to pick up women. After a conversation about how he was the nice guy always being overshadowed by the bad boys, I suggested that he not buy the book, but let me introduce him to my friend, Marjorie, instead.

Naturally, neither of them had wanted the other to know they were being set up, so I threw an entire party that they both happened to be invited to. The rest was history. They'd fallen in love instantly and hadn't spent a day apart since.

Of course, I left out the part about having to convince all the Pavers to come down to the city on a Friday for an elaborate pretend birthday party for myself. The whole party had come together in a day. I'd been pretending for both Clint and Marjorie's sakes that the party had been planned for weeks. It wasn't until after fifty Pavers had agreed to the act, that I'd realized that I had nowhere to throw said party.

Like a knight in shining armor, Rupert had ridden in on his white horse with a fantastic apartment in Downtown Dallas that his human friend let him borrow.

Thinking of Rupert stung a little until I remember the promise that I'd made to myself. As soon as the toasts were made and the cake was eaten, I'd leave the reception hall and finally open that envelope.

Two kisses, two hugs, and one heartfelt congratulation later, I was sailing through the night's sky, trying to find the perfect place to open my card. Even though I was alone, I still wanted the moment to be as perfect and romantic as possible. I'd land in a field of bluebonnets, lit up by a full moon.

I changed positions three times, finding the right one to see the card without squinting and to be the most comfortable as possible. I sat with my legs to my side bent at the knees with a perfect cushion of flowers to soften the blow right where my head would land if I were to fall back with glee.

Possible names scrolled across my mind, trying to imagine who it would be. The idea was baffling. There were so many guys that I'd never considered—never let myself consider.

Jeremy Castille, a handsome, happy-go-lucky Cupid twenty years further into his Hundred than I was. He'd always been so nice to me and offered me guidance when I was first starting out. I had never felt particularly drawn to him, but that didn't mean that I couldn't be.

Zach Flint, a shy Muse who occasionally joined Lana and me at our morning coffee spot. I had always assumed he found comfort in Lana's accepting nature, but maybe he'd been trying to get close to me the whole time.

Or could it be Simon Avery, a Cupid who had just finished his Hundred and still hadn't found his Fated? The idea was a little disheartening. I couldn't imagine what we'd have in common, but I didn't know him well at all.

Shaking my head, not wanting someone I'd have so little time with, I moved on to the next possibility.

William Djokic, an Oracle that I knew loved each and every baby he whispered to. I kind of liked the idea of being with someone who loved his job as much as I loved mine.

Ray Chu was another guy who loved his work. He was an Elve who loved giving people their second chance at life. He said that watching people live after they knew how close to dying they were put every day into perspective.

I clamped my teeth. I knew how sad he got though when he had to formulate a way for someone to die after having just found themselves at death's clutches. I knew I couldn't handle the sadness, so I dismissed all other Elves as possibilities.

Deciding that a Cupid really was the most likely choice, I focused only on them. Ian Fitzgerald, Jeriah Forbes, Dominic White—they were all of appropriate age, all handsome in their own right, all good guys. Any of them would make sense. Sure, I'd never felt a spark, but I'd had blinders on my whole life, not wanting to fall for the wrong guy.

Searching my mind for other eligible bachelors, I realized that maybe my Fated wasn't actually eligible, and that was why the Cupid's Kiss hadn't come yet. He could be married. Sure, divorce was rare amongst our kind, but sometimes a Paver was meant to be with one person for a little while to fulfill one aspect of Destiny, but later they are meant to be with someone else.

Another possibility was one that I'd thought of before. My Fated may not have been born yet. People said I was naïve, maybe I was supposed to remain young at heart until my Fated reached maturity, and then we'd be matched. With that awkward possibility weirding me out, I jumped to another option.

Maybe the man I was supposed to end up with wasn't even from my territory. Sometimes a region had too many of one type of Paver in their jurisdiction so they'd send a few to other metroplexes that were in need of more bodies. The idea of a Cupid from another state or country was appealing. He might have an accent or a whole different way of thinking. I'd been assigned men from Israel, France, and Australia, all of them had taken my breath away the second they'd opened their mouths.

Excited and eager to know, I decided that wondering and trying to solve the mystery while I had the answer in my hands was silly. Turning the envelope over a couple of times, readying myself for The One's name, I steadied my breath.

I flipped the card and stared at the unbroken heart-shaped wax Seal. Exhaling, I pulled the Seal, careful not to break it so I could melt the wax like it'd never opened it. I closed my eyes while I opened the card, having done it so many times before, but when it contained someone else's Fated.

After a moment to calm my heart, I opened my eyes and read the name of the man I was to spend the rest of my life with.

Chapter Seventeen

$\mathcal{I}$ closed the envelope, counted to three, and then opened it again. The name was the same: Rupert Lovett. I used all my might to try to rip the card, wanting to shred it into pieces to rid the world of its existence. If I didn't acknowledge it, maybe it wouldn't be true.

The card didn't rip, however. Stupid magically re-enforced paper.

The mound of flowers that I'd previously anticipated falling into because of joy caught my head as I threw myself against it in anger.

"Ugh!" I screamed. Like a bad-tempered child not wanting to take a nap, I kicked my feet and pounded my fists into the ground. "Why?" I shouted. I didn't expect anyone to answer, but I found myself asking again, a little softer this time, "Why?"

Angry, throaty wails escaped my mouth as my feet and fists finally tired of their temper-tantrum. "Why?" I whined again, staring into the stars. "Why?" I whisper-asked the smallest one I could see.

❤

Waking up in a field full of longhorn cattle was a first for me. I could only imagine what I might look like if someone were here to witness it. I sat, in the dress I'd worn to the wedding—high heels and all—not five feet from a white steer with brown speckling. He was staring right at me. Beyond him, I counted seven more cattle of similar coloring. They looked at me curiously, without dangerous intentions, but I was terrified regardless.

Thanking Fate for giving me wings and a Veil, I disappeared as quickly as my reactions allow.

"Holy Cow!" I screamed as soon as I covered myself with my Veil. I hadn't been concentrating, so instead of throwing one just to hide me, I'd cast a big one, bringing everything within ten feet in with me.

"Holy Cow is right." Percy laughed.

"These cows don't have holes," Penny chimed in.

"From where I'm sitting, I see plenty of holes." Percy wrinkled his nose as he stared at a longhorn lifting his tail to swat flies off his back.

Each twin lounged on their own cow in a lazy, backward riding stance. Percy leaned forward, resting his chin on his palm, and Penny leaned all the way back, her feet crossed on her cow's rump.

"You two scared the daylights out of me. What are you doing here?" I didn't know how they were so comfortable with the enormous animals. The twins were so tiny, and the cows are so big, not to mention their enormous, sharp horns. I hovered above them all, frightened.

"You act like you weren't born and raised in Texas." Percy stroked his longhorn's coat.

"I wasn't. I was born and raised above Texas."

"Same thing," Penny said. As if to make her point, she used an imaginary lasso to catch a steer by its horns and tugged hard.

"What are you doing here?" I asked again.

"We could ask you the same thing." Percy raised his eyebrows.

"We don't need to though," Penny added for Percy's benefit more than for mine, judging by her tone.

"Don't act like you stumbled past me by chance. Texans or not, y'all aren't exactly the type to wake up and milk the cows."

Percy laughed so hard he fell off his cow. "You don't milk longhorns. They're boys."

"Whatever, you know what I mean. Don't change the subject. Why are you guys here?"

"We're working," Penny said.

"And you decided to stop in this exact field on your way to an assignment? On a Sunday?"

"No." Percy didn't elaborate.

I stuck out my chin, urging him to explain further.

"We are at our assignment," Penny said meaningfully.

"We're getting paid time and a half 'cause it's a Sunday," Percy said proudly.

All Sprites had Sundays off unless a person's Destiny was at risk of changing so quickly that their annoying services were justified. The schedule allowed people to have lazy Sundays, but hellacious Mondays. Sprites started early on Mondays to make up for lost time.

I looked around, trying to find the person they were assigned to torment today. I met both of their stares. "No way." I shook my head.

"Way," Penny apologized.

"Why?"

Percy somersaulted three times. On his final turn, he held up my opened assignment card, like a jester presenting his trick-card to his queen.

I felt blood rush to my cheeks, and I knew I was blushing. "You came all the way out here so I wouldn't forget some assignment's card? Can't they print another one?" I knew they knew that card was mine, but I hoped they wouldn't acknowledge it.

"Not just anyone's card." Penny's face is filled with pity. I knew she must hate being the one sent here to call me out.

Percy had no such feelings. "Your card!"

"Give it back!" I lunged at him but retracted because I get too close to a horn.

"Come and get it." Percy flew just out of my reach, dangling the card above my head.

"Give it to her." Penny sounded bored.

"Not before I read it."

"No, don't!" I knew I was giving him the reaction he wanted, but I couldn't help it.

"Why not?" He pouted.

"Aren't you going to tell us anyway?" Penny asked, pain in

her voice. We'd bonded the other night, and now, it seemed, she expected to be told all about my boy-gossip. If it were just Penny here with me, then I would gladly cry on her shoulder, but it wasn't.

I tried to tell her as much with my eyes. Out loud, I said, "No, I'm not."

Percy took on the same scorned look Penny wore. He and I hadn't bonded the other night though, so his hurt turned to anger. He pulled the card out of its envelope, eyes locked with mine the whole time, daring me to stop him.

"Wait!" I held my hand out. "I'll tell you."

Reluctantly, Percy pushed the card back into the envelope.

"But you have to tell me what you are supposed to prevent me from doing, and I just won't do it."

"No deal," Percy said.

At the exact same moment, Penny said, "We're supposed to keep you from telling him."

"From telling my Fated? Why?" I asked Penny.

"No." Percy stopped her from answering. "You tell us whose name is in here first."

I looked from Penny to Percy then back at Penny. "Penny." My face pulled into a tight frown, and I dropped my head to one side, willing her to figure it out so I wouldn't have to say his name aloud.

"No," she whispered. Her tiny arms were wrapped around me before I saw her coming. "It's him?"

"Who?" Percy flew into my sights.

"Not now, Percy," Penny told him.

"Right now," he argued.

"Just look," I said. I didn't want to hear his name as much as I didn't want to say it.

"I swear if you're all pissed off like this, and I find my name in here, I'm gonna throw a fit."

That made me laugh. Last night, I'd gone through every male name I could think of, and Percy hadn't even registered. I felt bad for that; he was someone's Fated, after all.

"Oh, shove off, it's not you." Penny released me from her grip to push Percy's shoulder.

I turned to look at him, wanting to see his reaction to

Rupert's name in my card.

His eyes widened, then he recovered his surprise quickly. "I told you that you're in love with him."

"I am not!" I succeeded in snatching the card from him this time.

"Are too."

"Grow up!" Penny scolded him. "He was a real ass to Freya the other day."

"He's a real ass every day," Percy corrected her. "But, now you know you're meant to be, so just get over it."

"It's not that easy."

"She's not supposed to just get over it," Penny reminded him. "She isn't supposed to know he's her Fated yet. And he can't know either. Remember?"

"Do you know why?" I asked.

Sprites weren't supposed to have anything to do with Cupid business. Anti-Cupid business, like today? Yes. They were supposed to divert people from meeting at times by causing them to be so late that they miss their regular bus. Sometimes they'd lead them to find their boyfriend or girlfriend cheating on them so they'd become single and ready to meet their Fated. But they never knew the greater meeting behind it.

"We're never told anything cool like that." Percy pouted and crossed his arms.

"I don't know, know, like officially or anything. But I bet I can guess," Penny offered.

"Well, spit it out!"

Penny shrank away from me a little. I wasn't the type to demand anything from anyone. I was usually the happy-go-lucky type that believed in the bigger picture and accepted that things were out of my hands and what was meant to be would be and all of that. Now, I realized I'd only felt that way until Destiny started working itself on me.

I suddenly didn't want things to happen to me without knowing why. I was starting to understand why people had laughed at me and called me naïve so much. Life happening to you as opposed to making your life happen sucked, for lack of a more ladylike term.

"Sorry, I didn't mean to snip at you. What's your theory?" I regained control of my attitude.

"People don't always see us." Penny gestured between herself and Percy. "I mean even when we aren't Veiled. We kind of disappear into the background, and people don't think we listen. But, we do."

"Yeah, usually we only hit people in the head with the ball so they notice us," Percy added.

"Anyways." Penny rolled her eyes. "Even the big-wigs at all the HQs think we're too simple-minded to do anything with information that we may overhear so even they talk like we aren't there."

"Why does Freya care that Simon and Audrey are trying to get relocated to a less busy territory?" Percy asked, confused.

"That is not what I am getting at," Penny said. Maybe they're right about you being dim-witted after all."

"That is so not funny!" He dropped his Veil and appeared in front of the longhorn that Penny had made into a sofa. The longhorn startled and took a heavy jump to the side, tossing Penny onto the hard dirt.

After Penny slapped the dirt off her pants and settled on another cow-couch, she told me what she was getting at. "Like I was trying to say before I was so rudely interrupted, I have overheard upper-management discussing when they should give what assignments. You know as well as I do that most cards are cataloged to be given out on specific dates well in advance, but when someone's Destiny has been compromised so badly—"

"Like when a Cupid decides to not Kiss her assignments or steals their own Cupid card." Percy gave my two biggest mess-ups as examples.

Penny acted like she didn't hear him. "So badly that management has to take it upon themselves to decide how to proceed. My point is, we have eavesdropped, more than once, in these conversations and they are always concerned with timing."

"We know that," I said, disappointed. I had hopes that Penny would've given me true insight as to why Rupert couldn't know about us being Fated specifically.

"What you don't know is why." Penny smiled.

"Oh yeah, that's a good point." Percy clapped Penny's back. "Because people have free will!"

"We know that too," I moaned.

"Listen to her." Percy pointed at Penny.

"In school, they taught us that everyone has free will and everyone has a Destiny, right?"

"Right," I said, exasperated.

"And they tell us that people's free will keeps them from fulfilling their Destiny, right?"

I raised an eyebrow and nodded, hoping she'd get to the point soon.

"Pavers are supposed to push people back toward their Destiny. We Sprites do it by moving peoples' cars in the parking lot, and Cupids by Kissing their assignment. The Kiss only works as a magnet though, it forces people to meet and notice each other, but it doesn't force them to fall in love."

"But they always do," I said. "Sure, sometimes I have to play good-old-fashioned matchmaker, but people still fall in love with their Fated because their Fated is made for them, designed to be the perfect match for each person."

"Eeehh!" Percy made the classic game show noise used when a contestant guesses incorrectly.

"That is where we've been wrong all of this time," Penny said excitedly, changing her lazy position on the cow to a more eager perch on its back. "People can and do ignore Cupid's Kiss. If the timing is wrong, people use their free will to deny the Kiss. So management has to decide the best time for Fateds to be matched."

"I mean I know that, in theory, but I didn't know it actually happens."

"It happens all the time, and Destiny has to be re-written."

"Re-written?" The thought boggled my mind.

"So that's why Rupert can't know about our being Fated? The top-dog at Cupid HQ is afraid that if Rupert finds out he's supposed to be with me, he'll ignore the Kiss and choose not to be with me? Am I so bad?" I asked, surprised by how much the idea of Rupert denying me as his Fated hurt me. I was more than disappointed to see his name there, sure. But a sliver of me hoped that when he found out he was supposed to be with me that he'd be happy. I, of course, would still be upset for a long time but I figured that eventually I'd accept our Destiny and forgive him.

Penny flitted to my side and put her arm around me in an awkward hug. There was something unnatural about a person as small as her comforting anyone. But not as awkward as the pity-taps that Percy gave my head. I shook them both off.

"It's okay. I'm okay," I lied. "I need to go home and shower. I'll feel better when I don't smell like I slept in a pasture all night."

"But you can't tell," Penny reminded me.

"Don't worry. I won't be talking to Rupert. I don't want to actually witness him reject Cupid's Kiss."

Chapter Eighteen

$\mathcal{D}$espite my assurances, the twins flanked me all the way to the mini-city. "I told you, I'm not going to tell him," I said when I noticed they follow me to my apartment building instead of splitting off to their own.

"We're supposed to stay with you all day," Percy said.

"Why? I promised not to tell him."

"You can't tell anyone else either," Penny said shyly.

"No one? Not even Lana?"

"Specifically, not even Lana."

"Why not?" We'd reached my apartment door, but I didn't open it. I wanted to break down and wallow in self-pity. I couldn't do that with an audience.

"Again, I don't know anything for certain, but I can make an educated guess." Penny pulled a stray piece of grass from my hair.

"Then guess," I said.

"Lana has been on Team Rupert and Freya for a while now. She tried to make you believe in him. I think that the head Cupids think that if you tell her, she will tell him," Penny said.

"Tell him what?" Lana opened my apartment door from the inside. She'd been waiting in there for me all night, I'd bet.

"Nothing," the twins said as one.

"Nothing my ass. Somebody better tell me what's going on." Lana's stance was assertive and impatient, very unlike her usually mellow and chill demeanor.

"How much did you hear?" I asked.

"Enough to know that something is going on big enough that the bosses are involved, and they are making the three of you keep something from me."

The twins and I exchanged a three-way glance.

"Tell me. If it's about me, I deserve to know." Lana pulled my arm, and the rest of my body followed it into the apartment.

Lana closed the door behind me. The Sprites let themselves in, however, and all four of us crowded into my small apartment. My eyes flicked reflexively to the wall where Rupert had hung my picture frame along with the picture, flowers, and apology note. Pain washed through me when I saw the gifts were where I'd left them.

"If you were here, I wish you would have at least gotten rid of that stuff." I gestured to that side of the room without looking at it again.

"Why would I get rid of it? Rupert gave it to you. Freya, he told you he loves you. You have to believe him."

"Told you so," Penny sang quietly.

"Told her what?" Lana turned on the twins. "Is this what you were whispering about in the hallway? What does it have to do with me?"

"They're assigned to me today." I rolled my eyes. "They're supposed to make sure I don't tell anyone, especially you and one other person, that—"

Percy interrupted me. "Something. She can't tell you something."

Lana glanced at Percy, opened her mouth then thought better of it. "Okay, Cupid HQ stuff is important, I get that. If there is some big secret that for some reason they trusted y'all with, but they don't want me to know, I get it. I really do know how important all the Destiny stuff is."

"Good." I exhaled.

"That being said, someone better tell me what the secret is. I promise I won't tell."

Percy shook his head violently. "No. No. No. No. No. We failed at finding Freya in time, so she knows. And we know. That's three people who aren't supposed to know. We can't tell you because then you'll run off and tell him, and then we'll get our Veils revoked."

Lana's quick mind pieced it all together before Percy had even finished his rant. "You opened your card?" She smacked my arm. "We talked about this. You promised you'd return it. In fact—" Lana pulled out her phone, scrolling through and showing me our text conversation. "You told me you did return it."

"Yeah, well, I didn't. And I got all mad at Rupert and then went to this wedding where everyone was happy, and I got jealous, so I decided to open it. I thought that if I knew who I'm supposed to be with, then I would just accept it and be happy."

"Then you found out your Fated is Rupert and you got all mad." It wasn't a question.

Percy dropped the bouncy ball he'd been toying with. It made three dramatic thuds before anyone spoke.

Penny was the one to ask the obvious. "How did you know its Rupert?"

"It's obvious." Lana held my shoulders to ensure I was listening to her. "Freya, he's in love with you," she said slowly.

"No, he's not."

"Whatever. Believe what you want to believe. Just close your mind to the truth 'cause it's easier." Lana almost yelled.

Her tone shocked me. She was never angry. And she was certainly never mad at me. "What is your problem?" I snapped.

"My problem is that you're afraid of feeling. You talk all of this sunshine and rainbows talk, but when your sunshine and rainbows actually show up, you don't want to have anything to do with them." Lana glared at me as I processed her words. Were the sunshine and rainbows supposed to be Rupert?

I didn't get to ask her, because she turned on her heel, her billowing skirts chasing after her.

"Uh oh." Percy and Penny exchange looks.

"Freya," Penny said under her breath at the same time that Percy claimed Lana.

"Why are you following me?" Lana asked Percy.

"You know too much. Now I get to be your shadow all day long and make sure you keep your lips shut."

I wanted to snicker and crack a joke about how I didn't think Percy wanted Lana's lips to stay shut at all, that he wanted to kiss her lips, but I didn't. I could feel that this fight that I wasn't even aware that I was having with Lana was going to take a lot more than a distracting quip to make up.

The door closing behind Lana was like the sound of jail cell slamming shut. I was locked into this apartment of misery with my depressed state of mind and angry feelings and of course, with a hyper, eager, pity-filled, but over-all happy Sprite.

I looked at her. She'd already retrieved my caboodle of nail polish and waited for me on the couch. Today was going to be exhausting.

Chapter Nineteen

$\mathscr{P}$enny had finally fallen asleep. It seemed like it had taken forever. We'd spent the whole stupid day, playing makeup and trying on dresses. Normally, that would have been the most ideal way to spend a day off I could think of. Not that day though.

All I'd wanted to do was curl up in a little ball on my bed, listen to mopey music, and cry myself to sleep. I still couldn't even do that, because Penny had fallen asleep sideways on my bed, starfish style.

As quietly as possible, I snuck out, feeling bitter that I had to tip-toe out around my own apartment.

I didn't know where I was going. The Parched Paver was out. I would inevitably run into one of the two people I was avoiding most: Lana or Rupert.

She'd be there, waiting for me to come to my senses and talk to her about what I'd seen in the card. And I wanted to, but I was also hurt by what she'd said. "Sunshine and rainbows."

Then there was Rupert. He'd be there no doubt. Either drinking away his misery or distracting himself with Jacqueline or another boozed-up bimbo.

I physically winced at the memory of him kissing her.

I'd been pacing in front of my door long enough to warrant attention. Marisol, the Oracle who'd been pro-date, beckoned me forward with a crooked finger. "I have cookies."

I tried to school my face into the polite smile I usually flew around wearing, but it felt forced. "That's okay, Marisol. I don't have much of an appetite."

"The cookies are for me, not for you."

My smile snuck up on me, genuine.

"Come talk to a lonely old woman."

Guilt flooded me when I realized I'd been too distracted last week to visit her like I usually did on Sunday evenings and here it was Sunday again. "Just for a couple minutes."

She nodded, disappearing into her apartment, leaving the door open for me.

I closed it behind me. I smelled the cookies immediately. My nostrils widened to allow as much of the pleasant scent to flood me as possible. If I could smell this for the rest of my life, I might be distracted enough from my boy problems to be happy.

"You sit. I'll grab the milk."

She did as I said, letting me do the work for her. Poor Marisol, she'd never found someone to share her life with and help with the burdens of life. The least I could do was get the milk for her.

"You sure are good to an old bat like me."

"I'm just using you for your cookies," I said, swiping a gooey chocolate chip cookie off her Santa plate. It wasn't Christmas time, but Marisol was an odd one. If she wanted to use her Santa plate year-round, then I wasn't going to try and stop her.

"Tell me your worries, baby. I don't like that frown on your face. You know, if you hold it that way long enough, eventually it'll become permanent."

"Oh, I'll be okay. Nothing you need to worry about."

"I'm already worried. And if you don't tell me, I'll just concoct some stories in my head, trying to reason it out. Is your apartment infested with bees? Is that why you were standing outside your apartment? Or was there a bear inside?"

How did she suppose a bear would make its way to a cloud in the sky. "Nothing like that."

"Then it must be boys."

I laughed. "How did you figure that?"

"Because the only time I've ever looked as bent out of shape without being in the presence of a bear or bees, was because of boy drama."

"You had boy problems?" That was news to me. Marisol

was at least one-hundred-and-ninety and had never received Cupid's Kiss. But then I supposed, that was a problem in itself.

"Oh, honey." She grabbed my wrist.

Her cold, wrinkly hands felt familiar, and for an instant, I was brought back to a time before I'd stolen my Cupid's card and simply came to see Marisol to brighten her day.

"Just because I don't have a husband, doesn't mean I didn't have boy problems. I got myself into more trouble than a girl knew what to do with."

"Then why—?"

"Why am I alone?"

"Well, yeah." I offered a sideways frown. "If you don't mind me asking."

"Because I chose it this way."

I dunked my second cookie into the glass of milk I'd poured for her. "That's not possible. We don't get chose to be alone, just like we don't choose our Fated. It's all predetermined."

Her eyes twinkled as she leaned back in her seat. "That's what they want us to think."

"It's true. Why else would we exist if not to make Destiny come true."

"Oh, we all have a Destiny all right. And we're supposed to fulfill it. Those are the rules. But rules can be broken."

"No."

What Marisol was saying went against every belief I had. Went against everything I'd been taught my whole life. Each of us had an epic love that we were Destined for, and when the time came, we'd meet our Prince Charming and live out the rest of our lives in blissful happiness.

"Yes."

I shook my head slowly. "Even if we break the rules, someone comes behind us and fixes it."

"Exactly."

"Exactly what?"

"If we break the rules, Destiny is re-written. We're given a new one. One of our choosing."

The idea was preposterous. We couldn't choose our Destiny. We couldn't choose anything. It was all decided for us the moment we were conceived. Heck, before we were conceived.

From the beginning of time, every new life had been mapped out and brought into existence at the moment it was needed the most, to again, fill another's Destiny.

"So you're saying you chose your own Destiny?"

"That I did."

"And you chose to be alone?"

I watched as Marisol's eyes faded. Her head was pointed in my direction, but she was seeing past me, into a memory if I had to guess.

I crossed my left leg over my right, arranged my skirt, and switched legs. I felt uncomfortable like I was intruding on her while she relived a moment in the past.

"If I had my first choice, I'd be married. Married to Juan Lopez." Her eyes focused on me, and she smiled dreamily. It was an odd sight on someone as old as her. "I loved him more than I loved myself. Still love him, always will."

"I don't recognize his name."

"He's been gone longer than you've been alive."

"I'm sorry, I didn't know. How'd he die?"

She let out a bittersweet laugh. "Oh, he's very much alive. Living out his retirement in the Keys of Florida with his wife."

Somehow, that made me feel worse. I returned the gesture she'd paid me earlier, putting my hand on her frail wrist.

She moved to hold my hand, gave it a weak squeeze, and waved me off.

"Don't look at me that way. I came to terms with it one-hundred-seventy-eight years ago."

"No disrespect, but if you're still counting the years, it doesn't seem like you've truly gotten over him."

"I never said I've gotten over him. In fact, I said I will always love him. But that doesn't mean I haven't accepted it."

"But why? Why waste your heart on someone who loves someone else?"

She held her own hands, taking turns gripping one in the other. "Because he was in love with me until his Kiss. We were given our Kisses at the same moment in the same place. The four of us were having drinks, Juan, Emily, Theo, and I. Two of our friends, Cupids we'd trained with, appeared.

"I'd known why they were there the moment I saw their

faces. Beverly, my life-long friend, had sadness in her eyes. She told me she was sorry just before she'd Kissed me." Marisol blinked away tears before she continued. "I fought it. Theo was a lovely man, could have made me happy, but he wasn't Juan. Juan hadn't seen the Kiss coming though, he'd been blindsided and had been unaware of what was happening. One moment he was holding my hand, the next he'd Sealed the Kiss with Emily."

"Marisol, I'm so sorry."

"Me too, honey."

"If you knew he Sealed the Kiss with Emily, why didn't you let yourself Seal it with Theo?"

"Because I knew what love felt like. Real love, the kind in those movies you're always watching. I knew I'd never feel that way about Theo as I'd felt for Juan."

"But the Kiss—"

"Yes, the Kiss would work, it would have forged an unbreakable bond between Theo and me, but I knew I'd never forget the love I had with My Juan."

"So you made the decision when you were what, twenty, to never love again?"

She shook her head. "No. I thought I'd find love again. And a couple of times I came close, but nothing compared to Juan. Eventually, I stopped looking."

My heart fell into my stomach. How could she have lived so long being so alone?

"Do you regret it?"

"Not even once."

"But you said you could have been happy with Theo."

"But Theo would have never met Diane. They met down in the lower city on a job. She had to fly in from Chicago to Kiss her assignment because she missed him at the airport. Theo and Diane met and fell in true love. He proposed, and they've had nine beautiful babies."

I was on my fourth cookie before I found what to say. "And you've been happy?"

"More than happy. The only thing I've ever loved as much as Juan is my work. Telling those babies their amazing futures fulfills me every day. If I would have been with Theo and had nine kids to take care of, I wouldn't have gotten to do what I love."

"Why did you tell me all of this?"

"So you'd go out and chose your own Destiny."

Chapter Twenty

*P*enny was wound up as tight as a Jack in the Box ready to spring loose when I walked into my apartment.

"Where the hell were you?" She flew to me so fast I jumped back.

"I was just—"

"Do you have any idea how worried I was?"

"I'm sorry I worr—"

"I was terrified!"

"I was trying to say—"

"I thought I was going to lose my job. I thought Percy was going to lose his. When I called him, and he said you weren't with him and Lana, I thought there was no way you could be stupid enough to go see Rupert."

"I didn't go see—"

"Then when he said he hadn't seen you either, I thought maybe you—"

"You talked to Rupert?"

The tables had turned. I was the one on the offensive now.

Penny's wings propelled her back. Shame washed over her features. "I … I … I just thought."

"You just thought I was an idiot?"

"You were really upset, and I thought maybe you went to him and told him about the card so that he'd get upset and throw off Destiny or something."

I washed a hand over my face and tried to calm down. I hadn't thought to do that, but I kinda wished I would have. I still could. Marisol had just told me to take Destiny by the horns and steer it how I wanted.

I didn't want to do it that way though. Not by getting Penny, Percy and myself in big trouble.

"I was across the hall at Marisol's. I wasn't off ruining our lives."

Relief washed over Penny, and she let her wings slow until she landed. "Did you tell her what was going on?"

"No. I mean I told her I had boy problems but didn't go into detail."

"Did she make you feel better?"

"A little," I admitted.

"That's good." She smiled. "Let's go to bed. It's getting late."

I let her guide me back to my room. No matter how many times I promised her I wouldn't leave the apartment until she came back in the morning, she wouldn't agree to leave my side.

It was the same way when woke the next morning. Apparently, the Sprites had been assigned to my case until their HQ determined otherwise.

Penny followed me the next morning to the coffee-shop Lana and I always met in the mornings.

Lana didn't show. And I didn't call her to ask why not.

Penny offered to ask Percy what was up with her since he was her personal spy all day, but I declined.

I was up to my wings in failed Kisses, so I'd called in sick — again — and prepared myself for a long day of Cupid clean-up. Starting with Carrie and Adam.

Penny did not like that.

"You should start with an easier couple," she said, flying in front me.

"This is the easiest couple," I argued. "I just have to plant their Kisses and go. The other couples will take a lot of work."

I didn't even know how to go about re-Kissing someone. If it were as easy as Kissing Carmen again, it would have worked the first time. And I didn't even know what had happened to Jenny and Ivan. Had he used his free will and decided not to Kiss her, or had he been Kissed already? And if so, who was messing with my couples?

It had been a question brimming in my mind, but I'd been so distracted by Rupert that I hadn't let myself fully investigate. I'd wanted to write it off as a fluke.

As I got closer to Carrie's shop, Penny hovered next to me, as close as a sleazeball on a hot waitress, all day, but she didn't say much. I was glad she sensed my need to be alone with my own thoughts.

It took all my self-control to go to Carrie. I was so close to Adam, could almost feel how close to him I was with every minute we were in Denton. But I shoved the crazy thoughts aside, knowing what I needed to do.

When we arrived at Carrie's furniture store though, Penny threw a fit about me wanting to go in and see her, unVeiled. "This is a perfect example of what I'm supposed to be preventing you from doing."

"No. You're supposed to keep me from telling Rupert. And I'm not."

There was guilt behind her frown.

"There's something else you aren't telling me?"

"I didn't say that."

"What is it?"

"I can't tell you. Just promise me you'll stay Veiled?"

"No." I popped out of my Veil, knowing she'd stay in hers. Sprites were extremely hesitant about being seen because they usually weren't there to make people's day. And she'd come particularly unprepared today, dressed in her jammies and wearing a ball cap to hide her hair.

She grabbed onto my dress, trying to fly backward with me. But I was a lot heavier with my wings tucked away and unable to fly without the Veil.

My phone buzzed in my purse. I ignored it, knowing I'd only find a text written in all capital letters, warning me not to do what I was doing.

If she was angry with me before, she was furious when I came back out of the shop three hours later, with a new, freshly painted picture frame, and without Kissing Carrie. Her in the Veil and me not, all she could do was throw things at me and rage text.

I ordered my very first Uber and took the car all the way to

Adam's street in blessed peace and quiet.

The city looked so different from a car window than it did from a bird's eye view. Instead of rooftops and tree leaves, I saw front doors and tree trunks. Not to mention I was relaxed, leaning in a cushioned seat and resting my wings. I'd have to stop eating so many of Marisol's cookies if I went and made a habit out of riding in cars instead of flying over the metroplex.

The silence was shattered by my own laughter when I was forced to Veil myself for my time at Adam's house.

Penny's hat was missing, and her green-tipped hair darted in every direction. Her face was purple with rage.

"Don't you dare laugh at me," she spat, frantically trying to plaster her hair to her head.

"What happened to you?"

"You! You slammed the edge of my pants in the door. With me on the outside. I had to hold onto the luggage rack and air-ski the whole way. Thank Destiny there was no traffic, or I would have been a Penny Pancake."

I was glad for the Veil when I let out my next laugh. I sounded like a hysterical bear clawing and pleading for breath.

"Why didn't you Kiss her?" she asked when my laughs were more manageable.

I'd been asking myself that the whole ride to Adam's. I'd been so close, right there. All I had to do what excuse myself to use the restroom, Veil myself so I could plant the Kiss, and return minutes later with her none the wiser. But when the time had come, I couldn't. "She was talking about how happy she was to be single, and that she wasn't in a hurry to settle down."

"Uh, yeah, because she hasn't met Adam yet. Because you haven't done your damn job!"

I shrugged. "If they're meant to be, they'll fall in love. I'll give them a little push, but I'm not Kissing them."

"Oh no. You are not the person who gets to make these decisions, Freya."

I lifted off my feet and flew to the back of Adam's house. Penny followed, cursing the whole trip.

"So now what? Why even bother to come here if you're acting all high and mighty, deciding people's Fates?"

"I know what I'm doing," I said.

"And what is that, exactly? Why are we here?"

That's when Adam walked into view. His jeans hanging low on his hips. Shirtless.

"Oh." Penny's word was airy, and her grip on my arm loosened. "That's why."

He opened the back door, releasing an excited Ruby to the wilds of the backyard. She went bananas, jumping in circles trying to get to me.

"What is he doing?" Penny asked.

"She," I corrected. "She is Ruby. And she loves me."

"Oh, my Fates, Freya! The dog knows you?"

I made an ashamed, yet unapologetic face in her direction. "Not really. She's never seen me or anything. But she knows my scent."

"Why does she does she know your scent?" I'd never heard Penny's voice so low.

"I may or may not have fallen asleep on Adam's couch, and she may or may not have curled up on my lap."

"You're going to get me so fired."

Adam came into the yard to see what had Ruby all riled up. "You see a bug or something?" He chuckled at Ruby, patting her flanks to get her to calm down.

She wasn't having it. She started barking.

"Ruby." He snapped his fingers. "Trying to tick off the neighbors?"

When she still didn't settle down, I lowered myself and patted her head as inconspicuously as possible.

She calmed, sitting down and enjoying my praise.

Penny, who'd been even higher than me, lowered herself to mine and Ruby's level. As soon as she was within smelling range, Ruby's demeanor changed. Her lip curled, and she let a warning growl rumble through her chest.

Penny skyrocketed backward, acting as if Ruby had bitten her.

"You need help," Adam said walking away from his dog who probably looked insane. He left the door open. I really loved that habit of his.

I flew into the open door, Ruby trailing behind me, tail

wagging. Penny, who'd been on my wings all day, stayed behind.

"That's a good doggie," I said, getting in her face and rolling her floppy ears in my hand when I was sure Adam wasn't looking.

"Kiss him and let's go," Penny called from the doorway.

I sat on the couch.

Adam was watching a remodel show on HTV with his sketchbook in hand. I got as close as I could without him able to detect the cushions shifting underneath me.

He'd quickly drawn the shell of the kitchen on the TV as they showed the before pictures. I was mesmerized by his hands flying about the page, making perfect, straight lines and proportioned, little rectangles.

By the time the show had come to an end, Adam had drawn a detailed plan of what he would have done to the kitchen. He'd paid closest attention to the cabinetry, giving them depth and detail I could visualize.

When he was satisfied with his work, he sat the sketchpad in his lap and leaned back against the couch letting out a satisfied sigh. The force of his motion sent my hair flying about my face.

His nostrils expanded, and he breathed in deeply. He looked toward me and leaned in close.

I held my breath.

He had freckles on his nose. Cute, tiny, freckles.

He was so close. Close enough to kiss. I should Kiss him. I felt like I needed to kiss him, but not in a Cupid way. But the need to press my lips to his was too great. I'd wanted to give Carrie her free will, truly believed I could make them fall for each other organically. But I had to know, at least once, what his lips would feel like on mine.

No longer in control of myself, I leaned forward the slightest amount. I closed my eyes and let our lips brush.

I felt him flinch and back away.

I opened my eyes, looking for the blue sparks indicating my job was done. There weren't any.

He blinked a few times and shook his head.

Where were the sparks?

Penny's voice rang through the living room. "Finally, you

did it. Can we go now?"

Surprised to see her in the house, I looked around for Ruby. Had Penny won the dog over?

"Where's Ruby?"

Penny lowered her head in guilt.

"What did you do?"

"The gate just sort of unlatched itself. And then a Frisbee just sort of, flew out in the street."

"You let Ruby out of the yard?" I was in the air, flying at her.

"She was gonna eat me if I came inside."

"Penny!"

"She seems like a good dog. I'm sure she'll come back."

Chapter Twenty-One

$\mathscr{I}$ found Ruby rolling in a ditch, two streets over. Covered in mud and pleased with herself, she was ecstatic to finally see the body that matched my scent.

I knew I should have scolded her for caking herself with dirt and for running out of her gate, but it wasn't her fault Penny was a Sprite to her core.

I got on my knees and petted her as much as I could without getting filthy. I should've just hugged her though, because as soon as the excitement of seeing me was over, she shook the mud off her, flinging it all over me. My pink dress had just gotten brown polka-dots.

I'd planned on putting her back in the yard with hopes Adam hadn't noticed her absence, but then I heard her tags jingling. Looking at them, I discovered Adam's address was etched into the metal for this very reason.

An acorn hit my nose. Penny had figured out what I planned.

A pleased smile spread proudly across my face. "You have no one to thank but yourself."

Adam answered the door right away. He saw Ruby first and looked behind him, clearly expecting his dog to be in the room with him, and this dog to be one who simply looked a lot like her.

"Ruby? How'd you get out …" His words trailed away when he saw me. "Dirty Shirley?"

I let out an embarrassing giggle. "Dirty Freya, actually."

His lip ticked.

"Oh, God. That sounded … I'm sorry. Freya. Clean, not

dirty, Freya."

He pointed to my dress.

"Well, I'm dirty, obviously, but I'm not … dirty." I blew an exasperated breath out of my lips. "I found your dog. Or … whoever's dog this is. Your address is on her collar."

"Thanks. I have no idea how she got out. She's never done that before."

"Sometimes things happen we can't explain."

"I'm rude. Come in."

"Oh, I don't want to intrude. I was just bringing her back." Remembering the dog, I released Ruby's collar from my grip.

Adam and I watched as she bounded off into the backyard. To roll in more mud, or chase Penny, I didn't know.

While Adam's head was still turned toward the back door, I mouthed to Penny to make sure the gate was closed.

"Come on," he said, stepping out of the doorway. "At least borrow my bathroom and clean yourself off."

"It's really not a big deal."

"Please. You brought my girl back, the least I can do is let you get cleaned up. She got you pretty good."

I followed him to the bathroom in the hallway, proud of how well I feigned ignorance at his house's layout.

"Where'd you find her anyway?" he asked from down the hall.

I turned off the water when the mud was off my face and answered him, reapplying my lipstick. "A couple streets over."

"You live around here?"

I winced. I hadn't thought about why I'd be walking around a neighborhood in the middle of the day. It wasn't like I could tell him I was jogging, not with the dress and heels.

"I was waiting for an Uber ride outside my friend's house when I saw her."

"I'm surprised she let you bring her back. She doesn't like strangers." His voice came from the doorway and startled me.

I dropped my lipstick in the sink. The bright red left a mark on his porcelain sink. I tried to wipe it away, but it smudged into a pink blob. "Sorry."

"No worries. I have stuff to clean it with."

He stayed in the doorway. I could feel him looking at my

reflection, so I busied myself by continuing to scrub at the stain.

"Here," he finally spoke, "put these on so we can wash that dress. It looks too nice to leave stained." He was holding clothes out to me.

I shook my head. "Really. Not necessary. This is an old rag, not worth it."

He met my eyes and extended the clothes further.

"Not taking no for an answer." He set the clothes on the sink and pulled the door closed behind him.

Left alone in the bathroom, I didn't know what to do other than change into his clothes.

I squinted at my reflection. I honestly couldn't remember the last time I'd seen myself in shorts. Pants were a once a year thing, but shorts? It had to have been ten years since I'd worn shorts. And this was particularly comical because they were boy's shorts and not the cute little panties. The shirt did nothing for my figure. I had curves, real ones, but if they were hidden under baggy clothes, I was left looking heavyset rather than voluptuous.

I left the bathroom feeling self-conscious and frumpy.

"Thanks for the clothes," I said when I made it into the kitchen.

Adam had his back to me at the counter. He'd put a shirt on—sigh—and a cap rested backward on his head. "No prob. I'd offer you a beer, but I know you wouldn't want it," he said, turning toward me. "So, all I have is sweet tea."

He held two glasses of iced tea in his hands and had a big, amused smile on his face.

"Don't you dare laugh at me. You're a giant, and this shirt swallowed me whole."

He came over, handing me the tea. "I'm not laughing at how you look in my clothes, I promise."

"Then what are you laughing at me for?"

He kicked my foot.

I looked down and found I'd stepped back into my pink pumps. "Oh." I laughed too.

"You're not going to take them off?"

I knew I should, I looked silly, but I hadn't gotten a pedicure this month, and the polish was chipping off my toes. "Nope."

"All right," he said, shaking his head. "I don't know how you girls do it. Don't your feet hurt?"

Oh, they hurt. I did more actually walking in them today than I was used to, usually giving my feet a break when I flew. I couldn't tell him that part of the truth though.

"I actually wear them so often that I pretty much walk on my tiptoes even when I'm barefoot. It's kind of funny looking."

"Now I have to see."

I pursed my lips, pretending to think about it for a minute. "Nope."

We sat down at his kitchen table. I stirred my drink nervously. He passed a piece of ice back and forth in his mouth. We both started to speak at the same time to break the silence.

"You go first," I said. I hadn't even known what I was going to say.

"I was just going to say how funny it is that you're here. I mean, I'm glad. Just funny."

Not knowing what else to do, I agreed by way of a giggle.

"I was pretty bummed when you left so fast the other night."

"Really?" The spoon made a clanking noise when I dropped it into the tea.

"Yeah. I mean I know it looked like I was with that girl."

"Miss with a Twist?"

He rolled his eyes. "Yeah, her. But I wasn't like with her, ya know. She's just someone my friends keep trying to set me up with."

"She's pretty," I said, looking down at my glass.

"If you're into that sort of thing, I guess."

"That sort of thing? The pretty blonde with a good body thing?"

"The Queen Bee sorta thing." I looked up to see him swallow. "But blondes aren't my type regardless."

"What is your type?"

"Bubbly brunettes with big smiles."

I couldn't help the big smile that hopped onto my face. "Good to know."

I felt a swish of air by my side and caught the tea glass just before it toppled over. Penny was here to ruin the moment.

"I should probably go," I said, standing.

He got to his feet. "We haven't even soaked your dress yet."

"Right …" I let the word trail off. It would have been silly to change into his clothes for the sake of washing my dress and leaving without having done it.

"And didn't you say you'd left with an Uber on the way? Did you need a ride? We could hang out for a bit, and I can take you home when your dress is dry."

I tried to hide a wince at the thought of my dress tumbling in the drier.

My left knee buckled under me from a nudge from Penny, reminding me she was still here, and I was misbehaving.

"Or did you have somewhere you needed to be? I could take you wherever and you can come back and get the dress later? Tonight, or tomorrow night? Or I can bring it to you when it's ready."

Penny tugged one of my curls at the base of my neck.

"I guess I can back tomorrow night."

That hadn't been what Penny wanted me to say judging by the extra-hard hair pull.

"Good."

I felt his smile down to my toes.

"I can make breakfast." He laughed. "I mean dinner. Although I can make breakfast too." He grimaced. "That sounded bad. I mean I'm capable of making both breakfast and dinner. I wasn't trying to imply that you'd be here for both dinner and then breakfast." He chuckled, scratching his neck. "I'm gonna shut up."

I bit my bottom lip to keep from laughing. "I knew what you meant."

"I haven't been in the dating world in a long time, and I'm kind of a rambling idiot." His eyes widened. "I didn't mean that it was a date. Not necessarily. But it could be. You know, if you want."

I put him out of his misery. "I will be happy to come over for dinner tomorrow." I steadied myself for a jab in the ribs from Penny, but it didn't come. I heard Ruby barking in the back and figured Penny had gotten distracted. "For a date."

Chapter Twenty-Two

$\mathcal{I}$ had a lot of explaining to do. I had Adam drop me off at the coffee shop I'd noticed next to Carrie's store and told him I was meeting a friend there.

It didn't turn out to be as big of a lie as I'd thought.

Lana was waiting for me, looking like a ticked off tiger. Literally. She was wearing a black and orange striped maxi dress, and her red-orange dreadlocks fell wildly around her shoulders, making her look feral. The scowl. It was intense.

I expected her to roar when she spoke, but her voice came out lazy and sarcastic. "You look better than ever."

I rolled my eyes at her sarcasm. "It's a long story."

"You better start telling it, because from where I sit, it looks like you got dropped off by a human guy, and you're wearing his clothes."

"Well," I sighed. "That's the short version."

"Freya. I swear if you tell me that you crossed that line."

"Relax. Penny let his dog lose, and she got mud all over me. He let me borrow his clothes."

"Borrow implies that you'll see him again to return them."

I took a drink from her coffee to buy myself time. When I was taking too long, she pulled it from my lips.

"I have to go back anyway. The Kiss didn't work."

"What do you mean, the Kiss didn't work?"

"I mean what I said. I leaned in. I puckered. I Kissed. And nothing. No sparks."

Lana met my gaze meaningfully. "You were Veiled, right? Kissing him as a Cupid, and not as Freya, the girl?"

"Well, yeah. Wait. Would that matter?"

She lifted an impatient hand. "Of course it matters. How do you think Rupert is able to go around kissing whoever he wants for the fun of it?"

"Don't talk about him," I snapped, trying to ignore the stab his name caused in my chest. All day, pieces of our last conversation had tried to penetrate my thoughts, but each time, I banished them, opting to think of Adam instead. But hearing his name spoken was too much. The words he'd said, I think I love you were in my mind. Jumping back to the point of the conversation, I said, "We aren't Veiled in the Cloud."

"The Cloud is Veiled, duh," Percy said, rolling his eyes.

"Well, it doesn't matter, because I was Veiled."

"What about her Kiss?" Lana asked. "Did that work?"

I stared at a menu board on the wall.

"Freya?" Lana said.

"She didn't do it," Penny said.

I snapped my head at her. "Penny?"

"You said she was at the girl's shop earlier," Percy said.

"I said she was with Carrie at the shop. I didn't say she Kissed her."

Lana breathed calming breaths through her nose. "You're giving me a headache." She stood, leaving her chair and her unfinished coffee. "Let's go."

"Where?"

"To Carrie. I'm going to stand there until you Kiss her. I'll force you if I have to."

A group of kids drinking from paper cups looked at us curiously. I was sure they thought I was some sort of weird prostitute getting yelled at by my Mistress for not sealing the deal.

"What's the point?" I asked, lowering my voice. "His Kiss didn't work so it won't do anything to her. And then I won't be able to Kiss anyone for twenty-four hours. And I still have to fix my other couples."

"You haven't fixed them, yet? Freya, you're going to be in so much trouble." She turned on Penny. "I thought you were supposed to be looking out for her."

Penny raised her arms in defense.

"Whatever," Lana said, throwing her skirts behind her.

"Looks like I have to do everything myself."

I slinked behind her like a scolded dog. When we'd wedged ourselves between two buildings and were sure no one was paying attention, the four of us went invisible to the rest of the world.

"Stop talking to me like I'm your kid, Lana. I'm an adult." I pulled my arm from her grip.

"I'll stop treating you like a kid when you stop acting like one." She breathed roughly through her nose, once again reminding me of a wildcat. Eventually, her breathing steadied. "I'm sorry for bossing you around, Freya. But I'm not sorry for looking out for you."

"I don't need you to look out for me."

"Really?" she asked. "So I guess returning your card to the vault doesn't count for looking out for you. And spending the day fielding questions about your whereabouts doesn't count as looking out for you either?"

"You did that? You returned the card?"

"Yes. Percy knocked Daphne's flowers over on her computer, so I could sneak in and replace it."

"You didn't have to do that."

"Yes, we did. If they found out—"

"I know, I know. I'd get my Kiss revoked."

"They'd do worse than that. They'd take your Wings."

I looked at my feet. My shoes really did look ridiculous with the shorts. "Thank you."

"You're welcome," she said. "Now don't let the risk go to waste. Fly in there and Kiss Carrie. Maybe hers has to be first or something."

I knew that wasn't how the Kiss worked, but I didn't want to argue with her anymore. We flew the short distance to the shop, and all three of them followed me into the back door. Carrie was putting the last finishing touches on the dresser she'd been working on the first day I'd met her. With one last stroke of her paintbrush, she stepped back and admired her work.

It was perfect. I had no idea how she'd managed to turn the scratched wood into a dresser fit to be in a showroom, but she'd done it.

Not wanting to waste any more time, or risk being pushed by Percy, I lifted my wings, preparing myself to Kiss her.

But before I could close the distance, a cloud of pink sparks flew from her lips. They raised above her head, swirling into a heart, and then darted away, searching for their match.

"Don't just stand there," Percy said, pushing me like I knew he would.

"I can't," I said, pointing to the space the sparks had just been. As a Cupid, I was the only of us that could see it. "She … they … someone just Kissed her."

"What do you mean?" Penny asked.

"Oh, no," Lana said.

"Oh, no? Why oh, no?" Percy looked between Lana and me.

"If someone else Kissed her," I said, "that must mean HQ figured out I hadn't done it."

"They must have sent someone else in your place," Lana said. "I told you they were asking questions."

"Oh, no," the twins said.

I knew I should have been worried about what it meant that HQ had sent another Cupid to do my job for me, but that's not what I cared about in that moment. All I knew was that Carrie had been Kissed, and that meant Adam had been too. Soon, maybe days, maybe hours, maybe minutes, Adam would find Carrie, and they'd Seal their Kiss. And I would be nothing more to him than the girl who'd brought back his dog.

♥

"Where are you going?" Lana asked, already following me.

Penny and Percy were a little late to react, but soon I heard them too. "Wait for us."

I was out the back door and zeroing in on my target. The pinks sparks weren't restricted to using doors and windows like we were. They took the most direct route to their destination, going through walls and cars and people like they weren't even there. They'd continue in a straight line until they met their match.

"She's following the sparks," Lana said.

They were getting away from me, but I saw the direction

they were heading, and soon they'd collide with the blue sparks, and a tether would be there, linking Carrie and Adam together until the Kiss was Sealed.

There was no way I could get to Adam before their sparks collided, but I could get to him before they Sealed the Kiss.

And then I'd do what?

I slowed my flight, realizing the absurdity in my actions just as a stream of blue crashed into the pink. Fireworks rained down onto the street below. And my heart fell with the embers.

Penny caught up to me first, slipping her hand into mine as I stopped flying. "It happened?"

"Yeah," I said nodding.

"What happened?" Percy asked.

"The connection was made." Lana came to my other side.

The cord of shimmery dust solidified, forming the tether. I rested my hand on it where the pink and blue came together in a knot. I couldn't feel it, but that didn't make it any less real. Gliding my hand along the air, I propelled forward.

"Freya," Lana said, voice, soft.

"I'm not going to do anything stupid," I said. "I'll stay Velied. I just want to see him."

The three of them whispered behind me, but I didn't pay attention to what they said. The sadness in my mind was too loud for me to have heard them anyway.

The cord grew thicker the closer I got to the source of the sparks. The closer I got to Adam.

They finally started to bow downward when we came upon a residential street. It wasn't one I'd recognized, but that didn't matter. Adam had been in his car when I'd seen him last, he could have gone anywhere after he dropped me off.

But as I got closer to the house the sparks were coming from, I didn't recognize the cars in the driveway. Adam's car hadn't been anything special, just a blue sedan, but I would have recognized it anywhere because it was his.

The doors to the house were closed, so I had to resort to window watching as I tried to find Adam in the house. The first few rooms I'd looked into were empty, but finally, I found a back bedroom with a woman in her fifties stood in front of a bed, sorting laundry. And lucky for me, the windows were old and thin.

"But I don't understand why you have to do it now," the woman said. She aimed her words at a door left slightly ajar. The trail of sparks led right inside.

He was in there. Adam. This must be his mother's house.

"I was hoping you'd help me with the lawn. We can replace the dresser a different day."

"And where are you going to put all that laundry?" A guy said, coming out of the bathroom and turning the light off. "If you leave it on the bed, Misty will knock it all off."

He wasn't Adam.

"That's him?" Lana asked.

"No," Penny said. "I've never seen him before."

"This isn't good," Percy said.

"Why not?" I asked, turning to him. "You said yourself that Destiny is re-written all the time. That must have been what happened here. Carrie was re-Fated to someone else."

No one gave me an answer. But I could sense what they were thinking. If Carrie was matched to someone else, that left Adam wide open for me.

Chapter Twenty-Three

The next day, I still wasn't able to shake my Sprite. Apparently, she'd been reassigned to me indefinitely.

"So what, you're my sidekick until Rupert and I are supposed to be Kissed?" I wished I'd thought to have looked at the date while I had the card. For all I knew, Penny was going to hang around a hundred years.

Who knew what was supposed to happen between Rupert and me before we were meant to be together. If they were waiting for him to stop being a scumbag, I might be as old as Marisol before that happened. I had to admit though, being assigned to Penny was a lot better than the alternative: being Kissed and being forced to spend my life with Rupert.

I wasn't going to let that happen. I'd let Destiny re-write itself like it had with Marisol. Even if it meant I spent the rest of my life falling in love with other people's love.

"Hardly," Penny said. "You're my sidekick." She pulled out a yellow envelope with the head of Kokopelli—the Native American god of trickery as its Seal. "You didn't think you were my only assignment, did you? I have to follow you around, but you have to follow me around too."

"I can't be a Sprite," I whined.

"You don't have to be a Sprite. Just a Sprite's sidekick."

I rolled my eyes, groaning. "I have way too much cleanup to do. I can't waste time throwing balls at people."

"Is that all you think I do?" Penny said, folding her arms across her chest.

I raised a brow, opening my assignment card for the day. We'd have to get to work if we had her assignment today too.

"Highland Park."

"I do so much more than throw balls." She sighed. "Sometimes anyways." She looked down at her card, frowning. "Arlington."

"You'd think they'd at least coordinate our assignments so we'd be in the same city."

"That would require the Sprites telling the Cupids that you stole your card, remember?"

"Not that I'm complaining, but why haven't they already told them?"

"Because they have faith in Percy and me." She stood proudly. "Plus, that would mean they'd have to play nicely with others, and Sprites aren't usually big on that."

"You think?"

She stuck her tongue at me. "Let's knock out yours cause it's closest and then head to Arlington for mine?"

Agreeing, I hoped out of my chair at the café. Lana hadn't met us because she'd been up late, finishing her assignment from yesterday. Guilt filled me. It was my fault she'd had to work late.

The members-only club was a sprawling piece of greenery surrounded by huge houses and old money. We landed in the parking lot. Still Veiled, I checked my reflection in a car's window to rearrange my wind-blown hair. I pulled red lipstick out of my purse and reapplied. "Perfect," I said, smacking my lips together.

"Why do you care?" Penny said.

I dropped my Veil in answer, wings receding as I did so.

"What is the point of that?" Penny texted me.

"There isn't one really," I said aloud. "I just like to interact with people. You wouldn't understand, Sprites don't play well with others, remember?"

Confident she was following me, but not really caring if she wasn't, I waltzed into the club, feeling smug.

A man at a front counter smiled at me and asked for my membership card.

Frowning, I tried on my sweetest smile. "I was hoping to look around and see if I wanted to join."

"I can arrange a time for a guided tour."

"That's okay. Can't I just take a peak around the place?"

He managed to keep his smile as he firmly told me no.

Back in the parking lot, Penny beamed at me with self-satisfaction as I huffed my Veil back on. "That was a waste of time."

She was right, and I didn't thank her for pointing it out.

This time when we entered the Club, we flew past the door guard. But not without Penny untying his shoes first.

"What was the point of that?" I asked, mimicking her question.

"There isn't one really. Sprites don't play well with others, remember?"

We laughed as I oriented myself with the place. The card just said I'd find Norma Washington here at this time today. Apparently, she was an avid tennis player. I'd Kissed my fair share of Cupids in clubs like these though, and I had a feeling I'd find Norma in the sauna or at a breakfast table and not on the courts.

I took a seat at one of the chairs at the small, round tables.

Penny plunked herself right on top of the white tablecloth.

"Shouldn't we be like, looking outside or something?"

I shook my head, inspecting a chipped nail.

A few moments later, I heard a gaggle of women enter the dining room. Norma was the leader of the group. I beamed at Penny.

"Okay, on with it then."

"Hold your horses," I said, moving to the next finger. "I like to learn a little something about them first. It helps me with the Sealing process in case they need guidance."

"Isn't that the point of the Kiss? It makes them drawn to each other or whatever?"

"Yes," I said," but it has to be Sealed within a week. And some people are shy, and it takes them a little longer than that."

"She doesn't look shy." Penny jutted her chin to the woman holding court at one of the breakfast tables. Norma had the attention of every woman in her posse.

"It was the craziest thing," Norma said. "Yesterday I was out to lunch with my sister for her fiftieth birthday, and Darren walked right up to me and asked me to go dinner with him that same night. I'd known him for years and had no interest in dating him what so ever, but yesterday, there was just something about him." She smiled like she recalled the way he looked in her memory. "I couldn't say no to him. We went to that great Thai food restaurant downtown you told me about, Susan. It was fantastic." She blushed. "But not as fantastic as what came after that. I didn't even go back to my house before coming here."

One of the women, Susan, I'd decided, cackled and waved her hands. "You are so bad!"

Norma nodded, hiding her face. "I know, I know."

"But what about Tom?" another woman asked. "I thought you'd had your eye on him for months now?"

"Tom who?" Norma slapped a hand over her mouth, laughing at her own joke.

I dragged my gaze from the women and looked down at my card. My face must have said, what I was thinking.

"Let me guess," Penny said. "Tom is supposed to be her fated?"

♥

Ruminating over yet another failed Kiss, I studied Penny as she paced in front of her victim. I mean assignment.

Brendan Rice was scheduled to receive his Kiss next month. Which meant he needed to be single.

"What do you think?" Penny asked, turning her head to get a better look at Brendan.

He was furiously pressing buttons on a game controller, eyebrows drawn, lips stern.

"Search through her Facebook account and leave an incriminating message for him to find, or throw her bra in the dryer?"

"Bra in the dryer?" I asked.

"Yeah, I've ended more than a couple relationships that way."

"I don't understand." I wrinkled my nose. "Dryers ruin bras, not relationships."

"Not true," she said, landing on his coffee table. There was a forgotten coffee mug, just begging to be knocked over by Penny's booted foot. "When a couple is unhappy, they fight over anything because they're so miserable. Usually, they pick fights about leaving the toilet seat open or putting things in weird spots when their cleaning. Those types of things make them grouchy and whiney. But if one of them does something as unforgivable as putting a bra in the dryer or turn off the PlayStation before saving the game, the fight gets real—name calling, old grudges come out, and then finally one of them admits how miserable the other makes them. Within a week, they're over."

"That's … horrible."

Penny shrugged. "You get the hearts and flowers part of the relationships, I get the fights and the breakups."

"No wonder you're so afraid to put yourself out there," I said.

"You're one to talk. You swore you wouldn't date until you found your Fated."

I couldn't argue. "Isn't there a less grueling way to split them up? I don't want to be a part of a slow death of a relationship."

"Like I said, we can search for some real dirt."

"That's not exactly ideal either."

"Oh, I know," Penny said, her eyes bright like she'd just been hit with a great idea. "Let's unVeil ourselves and explain to him that he needs to break up with his girlfriend because he is about to meet his one true love."

"Good idea," I said, already trying to find the words I'd use. Brendan's phone chimed. With a huff, he threw the controller on the table and pulled his phone from his pocket.

"That was a test, Freya. And you failed." She kicked the mug over.

The brown liquid spilled out, landing right on top of Brenden's PlayStation controller. He jumped from his seat, reaching to save it.

"Damn it!" he cursed, shaking it out and pressing buttons. Nothing happened. "Damn it!" he screamed again, turning it over and smacking it. Brown droplets poured from the creases of the buttons. "Natalie," he called. "How many times have I told you not to leave your half-drunk cups lying around?"

"I'm sorry," she said, stomping into the living room, not sounding very sorry at all. "How many times have I asked you not to tell me what the hell to do?"

Brendan was still desperately trying to force his controller to come back to life. "I wouldn't have to tell you what to do if you used common freaking sense." He threw the controller onto the couch. "You ruined my game." He gestured toward the TV. "I can't even save it without a working controller."

"Oh no." She turned her lips into an exaggerated frown. "You can't play your stupid game?" She walked right to the console and slammed her finger into the power button. "I guess you'll have to do something useful with your time. Like I don't know, pay attention to your girlfriend."

"What's that supposed to mean?"

"I don't know Brendan, rub whatever brain cells you still have left together and think about."

I closed my eyes, wishing I could shut my ears too. "I've seen enough," I said, "Can we go now?"

"Almost," Penny said, keeping her eyes on her assignment.

"Maybe I'd pay attention to my girlfriend if she was more interested in me than the mirror. You pay attention to yourself enough for the both of us."

Brendan's girlfriend backed up like he'd hit her. "Is that what you think of me? That I'm some self-centered bimbo?"

"That's what I know about you," he spat.

Silence filled the room like a tangible thing.

"Okay," Penny said, "we can go now."

We left through a bedroom window as quietly as we could, though I was sure we could have gone right through the front door and neither of them would have noticed.

"I need a drink," I said to Penny. "That was awful."

She nodded. "Just a day in the life."

We found a bar a few blocks from Brendan's place. It wasn't as snazzy as the Silverleaf or as cozy as the Parched Paver, but at least there wasn't karaoke.

"I don't know how you do that every day," I told Penny after the bartender slid a Dirty Shirley my way.

"It's not always that way." Penny sipped a blue-green

drink that smelled like skittles even from where I was sitting. "Actually, that was probably the worst one."

"How so?" I asked. "You made it sound like you watch people's hearts break regularly."

"Yeah, but that's with Percy. He always makes it kinda funny. He mimics their voices and makes faces behind their backs and stuff." She supplied me with an example of one of his faces. "With you though, it was just ... just sad. Percy helps me ignore the fact that their real people with real feelings. But you, you always care so much about people. I kinda felt like I was breaking your heart too."

I rubbed my chest. "You can't break something that's already broken."

"There you are," a new voice said.

Shanae, a beautiful, tall Cupid with tiny braids wrapped into a severe bun on top of her head stood next to me. Dressed in a pencil skirt and button-down blouse, holding a clipboard, she was all business.

"I've been looking for you, Freya."

Chapter Twenty-Four

 $\mathcal{T}$ he broken pieces of my heart worked together to pound in my chest.

"For me?"

"I don't see another Freya, do you?" She turned to the only other patron in the bar, a beefy man with more hair on his chin than on his head. "Is your name Freya, sir?"

His beady eyes sized her up. "What did you just ask me?"

"I'll take that as a no." Shanae plucked the glass from my hand and waited until the bartender took it from her. "I need you to come with me."

"Where are we going?" Penny asked, fishing money from the purse I'd given her the other night.

"I don't care where you go. I'm only here for Freya."

"I go where she goes," Penny said.

"No," I cut off whatever protest Penny was going to give Shanae. I didn't want her involved in this. Whatever this was. But I knew it couldn't be good. Shanae was our auditor. A senior Cupid who'd extended her Hundred to follow Cupids on their assignments to make sure we weren't cutting any corners or abusing our positions. If she was unVeiling herself to me, it wasn't good news.

We left a worried looking Penny alone at the bar, Veiling ourselves as soon as we were out of sight.

Shanae refused to answer any of my questions as I followed her to the Cloud, responding with a clipped, "You'll find out when we get there."

"There" turned out to be a conference room in Cupid Head Quarters.

Sitting in broad-backed leather chairs behind a long desk were four impatient looking Pavers. Maxine, the Cupid in charge of scheduling, tapped a pencil off her perfect teeth. Next to her was a Daphne, looking eager to see my head on a plate. Bill, the Oracle in charge of determining when Pavers were needed to intervene, shuffled papers—a large stack of papers—into a neat pile. And on the end, was Charlotte, the DFW branch manager; she'd been in charge for so long that no one even knew what her original classification had been. Or what her real age was for that matter, she looked not a day older than me.

"Take a seat," Charlotte said.

There was only one open seat on my side of the table, so shakily, I flew to it.

"Do you know why you're here?" she asked.

I could think of half a dozen reasons why I'd been pulled into a meeting like this, but I shook my head, not wanting to give a reason they didn't already know about.

"Why don't you take a stab at it," Charlotte said, leaving her chair and flying to the head of the table.

"Um," I racked my brain for the problem they were most likely to know about. And least likely to get my wings revoked. "Failure to report an UnSealed Kiss?"

"Not one UnSealed Kiss, but five UnSealed Kisses."

I counted on my hands under the table, trying to figure out how she'd gotten that number. There were Jenny and Ivan, the first couple and the one I'd been referring to. Carrie and Adam, who's Kiss wasn't Sealed because Carrie had been Kissed and matched to someone else. Carmen and Michael, who were in the same situation. And then today's couple, Norma and Tom, but I didn't know how they'd already learned about them. I didn't know who the fifth couple could possibly be.

"Not only were the Kisses not Sealed, but all five of them were Kissed to the wrong people." Charlotte folded her arms and perched herself on the edge of the table. "Care to explain how that happened?"

I was in massive trouble. I didn't need to see the joy on Daphne's face or disappointment in Maxine's eyes to know that. But I took a relieved breath that they didn't seem to know about my stolen Fated card. "Who is the fifth couple?"

Bill set his papers down and peered at me over thin-rimmed glasses. "I thought you only knew of one couple. Now you are aware of four?"

I smoothed my skirts. "I watched one couple—Jenny O'Connor and Ivan Rodriguez—fail to Seal their Kiss right in front of me."

"And you chose not to report it," Daphne said. "I promise, she didn't tell me."

As my supervisor, Daphne was the person I should have told immediately after witnessing the failed Kiss. She'd probably taken a lot of heat for not bringing it to Maxine's attention. That explained her smug look when I'd entered the room.

"So you've said." Maxine rolled her eyes. "Twenty times."

"And these other three instances you're privy to?" Bill asked.

"Carmen Mendoza and Michael Cummings. I Kissed Michael, and everything seemed right, but when I tried to Kiss Carmen, nothing happened. I tried again, but still nothing. And then she started going on about this new guy she'd recently started dating."

"And again, you chose not to report it," Daphne said.

"We know she didn't report anything, Daphne," Charlotte said.

Daphne sank lower in her seat. She looked like she wanted to Veil herself.

"The same thing happened today," I continued. "I was supposed to pair Norma Wells to Tom Schein, but when I got to Norma, she was telling her friends about recently falling for a man, and he wasn't Tom. When I Kissed her, it didn't work either."

"And the fourth?" Maxine asked.

I swallowed, not wanting to talk about Adam, but knew there was no way around it. "Carrie Timms and Adam Hannon. They were different." Different because they were the only couple I'd screwed up. "I Kissed Carrie the day I was assigned to her, and everything went fine. But I didn't Kiss Adam within twenty-four hours."

"And why not?" Bill waved his hand for me to give them more.

I didn't think because I fell asleep and was late for a date was going to fly over well. I racked my head for an answer that wouldn't result in my wings being chopped off right then.

"His dog."

"His dog?" Bill took his glasses off and massaged his temples.

"She wouldn't let me into the house." It had been true for Penny, so why not me?

Daphne opened her mouth to say something but shut it.

Feeling bad that I'd clearly gotten her into trouble, I added, "I didn't report it because I'd planned to try again the next day."

"But then you didn't show up to your shift." After speaking, Daphne looked to Charlotte to make sure she wasn't going to be chastised again.

"Yeah," I said. "I came down with something." I waited for Daphne to point out that I'd missed several days last week, but she remained quiet. Those days had been reported. "I did eventually go back though. But when I got to Carrie, another Cupid was already there."

"Who?" Maxine said. "No one else was assigned to Timms-Hannon."

"I ... I don't know," I stammered. "I'd thought ... I mean I'd assumed that y'all had figured out I hadn't completed the Kiss and sent someone else."

Charlotte looked to Maxine.

"I didn't reassign anyone."

"And you didn't see who it was?" Daphne asked.

I shook my head. "They were Veiled."

Charlotte glanced behind me. I followed her gaze and saw Shanae shake her head. "I wasn't with her that day."

That day? Had she been there other days?

Bill sifted through his papers, pulled one out, and wrote something on it. Underlining it twice. "And you don't know the fifth couple?"

"No." I listed the couples again, confirming. "Everyone else was successful."

"Did you check back on all your other couples?"

"Everyone that was a week from their Kiss, yes."

Charlotte nodded. "Owens-Keenen."

"They still have time," I said. "Plenty of time."

"They would have time if they weren't already Sealed to someone else."

"There's no way. I saw the sparks myself."

"Sparks aren't a Seal," Maxine said.

"Well, I know, but—"

"Tyler Owens Sealed as Kiss with Jenny O'Connor. And Molly Keenan with Michael Cummings."

"Those are terrible matches." Jenny was shy, intellectual, and loved country music. Tyler was eight years younger than her and played air guitar. I hadn't known much about Molly, but she was much too young to take on a man like Michael. "There's no way any of them will make each other happy."

"We know," Bill said, heaving a weary sigh. "It will be impossible to rewrite a happy Destiny for them."

There it was, proof from his mouth that Destiny could be rewritten. The twins and Marisol had said as much, but I wasn't sure I'd believed them.

"How did that happen?"

Maxine leaned forward on the table. "We were hoping you'd explain."

"I don't know."

"You didn't try to fix your mistakes? And accidentally match them to the wrong people?"

"I never even went back to any of them. It couldn't have even been an accident."

Not one of them looked like they believed me.

"What are we going to do with you?" Charlotte asked, walking instead of flying back to her chair. She took her time, getting comfortable in her seat before speaking again. "You know we have grounds to not only revoke your Kiss but take your Veil too?"

My wings spasmed. "Please don't do that. I'll do anything. Just, please. Don't take my Veil."

"We won't," Charlotte said.

I exhaled.

"Not yet," she continued. "You have two days to fix each and every mistake."

"She should at least be suspended," Maxine said.

"Oh, she is," Charlotte assured her. "Starting tomorrow, you will fix your mistakes. You'll have two days. And after that, you'll have your Kiss and Veil suspended for two weeks."

"But that means I won't be able to leave the Cloud."

"You will have no reason to leave the Cloud because you will not have assignments," Charlotte snapped.

Two weeks without being in the city? Two weeks without coffee with Lana? Two weeks without watching my couples?

"And if you don't fix all five couples, you'll have your Kiss and Wings revoked permanently. Without them, your Hundred will be terminated."

My Hundred? Without my hundred, I'd start aging again. I would be dead before Lana even turned nineteen. "I don't even know how to Break a Seal."

"We'll teach you, obviously," Daphne said.

"It's not a job you can do alone," Maxine said. "You'll have to work with another Cupid. Each of you will have to Kiss one in the Sealed pair at the exact same moment. That will break the Seal, and you will be able to Kiss them to the correct match again."

"This isn't fair," I said. "Someone else messed up the Kisses. I did what I was supposed to do."

"Maybe," Daphne said. "But maybe you were too distracted to notice you'd made terrible errors. But either way, you knew something went wrong and failed to report it."

I narrowed my eyes on her, furious she was pointing out my failings. Logically, I knew that as my supervisor, I'd made her look bad, but that didn't mean I'd forgotten what she'd said about my sisters and me. She thought we were all air-heads, and I'd gone and proved her right by losing control of my couples.

"And Freya," Charlotte added, "the new Kisses have to be Sealed within the two days."

I gulped. That wasn't going to be easy. It would be nearly impossible for most Cupids, but I'd had practice helping couples Seal their Kisses before. "I understand." I furrowed my brow. "Who am I working with?" I looked back at Shanae who'd been silent for most of the meeting, assuming she'd stuck around for this exact reason.

She shook her head, looking back at Charlotte.

Charlotte nodded her head, and Shanae flew to a door that connected to another conference room and opened it. "You can come in now."

Rupert walked into the room.

His hair was its usual gelled perfection, and his cologne was as strong as ever, but he'd lacked his typical arrogance when he walked in.

His eyes were on Shanae, and they left her to access the panel of Pavers in front of him. "Good afternoon," he said, nodding to each of them individually. They all gave him a curt nod, except Daphne. Her mouth hung open, and she turned to Maxine.

"I didn't know he was the Cupid she's working with," Daphne said.

"Why would you have?"

"Who am I working with?" he asked, and then he saw me. He took one step toward me but must have seen something in my eyes, because he stopped. "Freya."

I turned my head away from him.

"I know I'm not really in a position to haggle," I said to Charlotte.

"No, you aren't."

"But is there any way I can work with anyone else? Anyone."

Bill shook his head, but Maxine was the one who answered. "No. The schedule has been made. You're working with Rupert."

The rules were explained to us, I thought so anyway. They talked for a while and asked me if I understood, but I hadn't paid attention to anything they said.

"You start tomorrow," Charlotte said. "You two should come up with a game plan."

Chapter Twenty-Five

There was absolutely no way I was spending my last free night coming up with a game plan with Rupert. Of course, that's what I should have been doing. I definitely should not have been flying to Denton to have dinner with Adam. But there I was, landing in a gas station a few blocks away from his house so I could fix my windblown hair and reapply my makeup.

I walked the rest of the distance. My heartbeat sped up with each moment I took. I was doing it. I was paving my own Destiny. So what if they took my Veil. I'd get Lana to sneak me out of the Cloud. She'd carried heavier instruments than me around. She'd be able to fly me to the real city the city with people, and I'd be able to live out my human-lengthed life with Adam. We'd grow old together and be as cute as Glen and Anna, tending to our tomato plants.

And most importantly, I'd never have to see Rupert again.

Resolved more on the decision to write my own Destiny than ever, I lifted my hand to Adam's door and knocked.

Ruby barked, and I could hear the thud of her tail hit the door.

Not more than fifteen seconds later, Adam opened his door. He wore a shirt a lot like the one he'd worn at the bar, only this time it was a deeper blue, highlighting his eyes even more. They were huge, wide with … surprise?

"I hope I'm not too early," I said, realizing we hadn't set a time, just dinner.

"Freya?" Adam sealed the door to his side, presumably to prevent Ruby from getting out. She was whining and pushing between his legs with her snout. "What are you … right, dinner." He ran a hand through his hair, looking perplexed. "I'm sorry. I forgot."

Forgot? How could he have forgotten?

"Is it the food?" a girl's voice said from inside the house.

"It's just … a friend—the girl I told you about who brought Ruby back yesterday. I'll just be a second."

Ruby pushed the door wider, sliding through to get to me. She nuzzled my hand so I'd pet her.

With the opened door, I had a direct view to the inside of the house. Miss with a Twist stood proudly, holding a martini glass.

"Oh," I said, feeling my heart slide to my knees. "You have company."

"Yeah," Adam said, eyes full of apologies. I looked back at her and told her he'd be right back before joining Ruby and me on the patio, closing the door behind him. "I ran into Andie this morning on my walk with Ruby."

"And let me guess," I said, focusing my attention on Ruby so I wouldn't have to look at him. "You guys just clicked?"

He nodded. "Look, I'm so sorry. I know we had plans for dinner tonight. But we started talking and—"

"And one thing led to another and y'all shared an epic kiss."

"How did you know?"

I shrugged. "Lucky guess," I said swallowing back a huge lump.

"God, I feel like such a jerk. Man. You were coming for dinner," he said, using his thumb to point to the door. "We ordered Chinese. I'm sure there will enough to share, they always give so much."

I waved away the offer, unable to think of a single thing I'd rather do less. "No. That's okay. I get it." I turned my eyes toward him for the first time since I figured out what had happened, hoping the tears would stay in my eyes long enough for me to leave. "If I could just get my dress back, I'll be out of your hair."

"Oh right." Adam glanced at the closed door. "Is there any way I could get it back to you a different day? I would hate for Andie to get the wrong idea."

"Sure," I said. "I totally get it."

"Do you work around here? I could drop it off."

"Don't worry about it," I said turning away. "It's just a dress. I have more where that came from."

I kept my tears inside long enough to round the corner on the house so I could break down in private. Just before I Veiled myself, I saw Ruby pawing at the chain link fence. When I got close enough to her, her excited pants turned to whines.

Needing her love like a blanket, I Veiled myself and flew to her, taking her into my arms. She couldn't see me, but she could feel me, and she pushed her weight against me until I fell on the ground next to her.

She licked my tears as I cried. I cried for my heartbreak over Adam. I cried for my heartbreak over Rupert. I cried for my ruined career. I cried for the Destiny I'd wanted to make for myself.

Chapter Twenty-Six

Penny, Percy, and Lana were all waiting like anxious parents in my apartment when I got home. They sprung at me, each of them with their own questions.

Penny desperately wanted to know what happened with Shanae, and while Lana and Percy wanted to know that too, Lana was more interested in knowing where I was after I'd left HQ, claiming Rupert said I'd flown away without a word for him. Percy, ever the bluntest, wanted to make sure I hadn't included him or Penny in whatever alibi I'd made up for myself.

He still wasn't sure what I'd been in trouble for, but he knew it had been big.

I'd assured them all that no one was in trouble but me. Percy visibly relaxed and smiled at Penny and Lana, like all was good. Penny frowned at him and left him alone on the couch as she flitted to me. Lana was already at my side, smoothing my hair.

"It'll be okay," Lana said. "Rupert said he knows you two can fix everything."

I sobbed into her shoulder. She hugged me tighter.

"Did you go to your date?" Penny asked, trying to get in on the hug-fest.

I nodded into Lana's shoulder.

She stopped patting me. "Are you crazy?"

"We've known she's crazy for a while, haven't we?" Percy asked.

We all ignored him.

"I wanted. I needed." I couldn't finish my sentence.

How was I supposed to look Lana in the eye and tell her that I'd planned to throw my life up here away so I could go live in the human world with a guy I barely knew. All so what? I could have a choice? That was exactly it, I realized. But I'd known he'd already been Kissed to someone else. Charlotte had told me so. But I'd thought that if I was there, right there in front of him, that somehow, he'd forget whoever the girl was, and he'd chose me.

But of course, that had been stupid.

Penny pulled me into her arms. "What happened?"

I told them.

Penny's jaw fell. "The brat? He Sealed the Kiss with that brat?"

Percy awkwardly handed me a paper towel to wipe my face. "Yes." I blew my nose.

Lana had been careful while listening to my story, keeping judgment out of her tone when she asked clarifying questions, but wanting the details just the same. Percy had already explained the bar night to Lana while they'd been together, so Penny filled her in the blanks about the day at the house so I wouldn't have to.

I went a step further, explaining what Marisol had told me about writing her own Destiny. That seemed to explain my lapse in judgment to Lana, even if she didn't agree with it.

"But none of that matters now," I said, finally done crying, at least I'd hoped. "He's with that girl, and tomorrow I'll be superglued to Rupert's side, and I won't have a chance to make Adam fall in love with me anyways."

The room was quiet. No one knew what to say to me. I didn't think there was anything they could have said to make it better.

Lana spoke first. "*P.S. I Love You* or *Titanic*?" She held up the DVDs.

"*The Fault in Our Stars*," I said.

Percy groaned and left the room.

"Is that all I've had to do to shake him the whole time?" Penny asked. "Watch a chick-flick?"

He returned with a massive package of toilet paper from under my bathroom sink. "No one can use my shirt to wipe their snotty tears."

For the first time in my life, I hugged Percy.

♥

A knock at the door woke us up. Penny shot up from my lap, and Lana jumped to her feet, dropping my head on the couch. Percy kept on snoring.

The knock came again, and the three of us girls looked at each other.

Lana's phone went off. "It's Rupert."

"No," I said, grabbing my hair. "I'm not ready." Being forced to work with him was one thing, being forced to work with him while looking like a heartbroken slob was another entirely.

"I'll tell him to wait," Penny said, flying to the door. "In the hall."

Lana followed me into my bathroom as I hurried to get ready.

I needed a shower, there was no way around it, and Lana wasn't leaving me alone, so she sat on the toilet while I washed my hair.

"What I want to know," she said, "is who the hell is screwing with your assignments."

I'd wondered the same thing from the very beginning. But I'd been too wrapped up in my stupid, failing love life to pay enough attention. It was absolutely where my efforts should have been focused.

"I have no idea," I admitted, lathering conditioner into my hair. Rupert was going to have to wait while it set in. It was deep conditioning day, and he wasn't going to keep it from happening.

"One of your sisters?" Lana asked. "The younger one has always been out to get you, hasn't she?"

"Lada is too self-involved to come up with something like this. If it was one of my sisters, and I really don't think it is, it would have to be Damara. She's the only one smart enough, but she's always been the one to have my back the most."

"Not Isis?" Lana asked.

I thought about it. "She doesn't have a reason to want to sabotage my career, but if she did, she'd be more obvious about it, want me to know she was the cause of my misery."

"Then who?"

"The only person who's ever really given me trouble is Jacqueline, but she's not a Cupid so if she wanted to do something to me, she'd have to go about it another way."

"So what Cupids do we know that would want to get your Kiss revoked?"

I rinsed the conditioner. "And have enough free time to go around screwing my life up." I turned off the water. "He was there that day with Jenny and Ivan."

"Who?"

"Rupert. They were about to Seal the Kiss. I knew they were. And then they just didn't. Not even ten seconds later, Rupert showed up, brought me into his Veil, and stopped me from fixing it." I was so shocked by my discovery I forgot to wrap myself in a towel before I pulled back the shower curtain. "I'd been so involved with their Kiss that I'd started to let my Veil down. Rupert even said so. I wouldn't have been able to see Ivan's sparks or love cord without it."

Lana tossed me a towel. "You let your Veil down?"

I waved away her concern. "They didn't see me. Because Rupert had been there to Veil me again."

I didn't bother getting myself dressed-up like usual. I still did my makeup, I hadn't lost my mind, but I slapped my hair into a ponytail and threw on a simple purple dress I'd usually reserved for my days off.

Lana stopped me before I stormed out of the room. "What would Rupert gain from hurting your career like this? It would only push you further away from him. That's the last thing he wants, Freya."

"When are you going to get it out of your head, Lana? Rupert does not love me. He just wants to get me in bed. If I was trapped up here with Pavers only, he knows I'd eventually cave."

"That's ridiculous."

I thought so even as it came out of my mouth, but it was the only lead I had. And I would need the fury the idea filled me with if I was going to make it through these next two days without falling for Rupert. Because really, I was afraid of that more than getting my Veil revoked.

Chapter Twenty-Seven

$\mathscr{I}$ was glad for my newfound hatred for Rupert.

He stood on my doorstep with three dozen roses, red, pink, and white, all designed into a massive bouquet. He was as annoyingly handsome as ever, hair perfectly in place, polo starched, and smelling like he'd tried to drown himself in cologne. But he had circles under his eyes and a touch of stubble on his chin. His charming smile was nowhere to be seen.

"I'm sorry, Freya."

"Save it," I said, taking the flowers from him and tossing them at Penny. "I don't want to hear any of it."

I opened my mouth to tell him that I'd figured it out. That I knew he was the one who'd screwed up my assignments in the first place. But I stopped. If I told him of my suspicions, he'd tell me his ready-made excuse, and it would sound good and make sense, and I might believe him, and then where would that leave me? Broken-hearted, but no longer armed with my righteous anger.

"I assume you have a plan?" I asked.

He stammered. "I thought you would have a plan."

"You're kidding me?"

He pulled out a piece of paper from his pocket. It was folded just so into a square. He opened it as I flew off. "I have the names," he said, flying beside me. "Its pretty straightforward. We have to Kiss the mistaken couples at the exact same time, unSealing them, then when everyone is free to be Kissed again, you go back and Kiss them again, with the right couples this time, obviously."

I shot him a look. "Obviously." I zoomed between two Oracles, narrowly missing their shoulders. I smiled. Rupert would be too wide to make it.

He flew over them and sank to my level right at my side. "Then we do your magic and make them find each other, fall in love, and Seal the Kiss."

"I won't need you for anything other than the unSealing," I told him. "I can do the rest on my own."

He cleared his throat. "Actually, I have to stay with you the whole time."

"I know they said that, but I got it."

"Shanae will be auditing us."

"She's following us around?" I asked looking over my shoulder. I wouldn't be able to see her unless she wanted me to and I knew it, but I couldn't help the paranoid glances.

"Not the whole time, but she'll be stopping by randomly. If she sees you without me, she'll know I left you alone."

"And what? You'll get a slap on the wrist? You're their favorite Cupid. What are they going to do to you?" I swooped under a group of Sprites who were slowing to enter Sprite HQ.

"Not anymore," Rupert said when he caught up to me. He'd gotten caught among the Sprites just like I'd wanted him too. One of them had flipped his collar out of place. "I'm in trouble, too—that's why I'm assigned to you."

"I'm your punishment. That's real nice." I gave Cupid HQ a wide birth, not wanting to see Daphne or any of the other Cupids who knew I was in trouble.

"Freya, you know its not like that for me."

"What did you do?" I asked.

He sighed. "They found out I've been cheating the system, working with Cupids to get my assignments done faster."

I slowed just enough so I could look him in the eyes. "Cupids like Mariah." Then I was off, speeding as fast as my wings would carry me.

"Yeah," Rupert kept up, no problem what so ever. Darn.

"If she's in trouble too, why isn't she with us?"

"I wouldn't tell them who I've been working with."

There was some honor in that, but I wasn't going to tell him so. "We're going to do Cummings-Mendoza first," I said, catching a gust of wind that would take me straight to Michael's office.

♥

Since we weren't on usual assignments, we hadn't received Fated cards with each of our assignment's schedules neatly laid out for us. We had to locate each couple individually.

Lucky for us, Michael Cummings had brought Molly Keenan into his office that morning to show her around the place. Unluckily for us, he'd closed the door to his office so we couldn't swoop in and out unVeiled.

We'd hovered over his door for thirty minutes when Rupert said, "I think he's showing her more than his office."

I wrinkled my nose. "Gross." Michael wasn't old, only thirty-one, but Molly was so young, just nineteen. "That's it," I said, flying out of the building.

A moment later, Rupert was outside beside me, a smile wide on his face.

"Don't look so smug," I said, unVeiling myself when I was sure no one was around to see me blink into the parking lot.

Rupert appeared a second after me. "Are we playing house?"

I couldn't stand how cute he looked, eyebrows wagging and a half-smile playing on his lips. "I'm regretting this idea already," I said.

"We're newlyweds," Rupert said, wrapping a fallen curl around my ear. "Looking for our first home together. I'm thinking Flower Mound. Great schools."

I sharpened my glare on Rupert and smacked his hand away. I'd fantasized so many times about living on the ground, all with different scenarios, each time my imaginary-self had a family, we lived in Flower Mound.

"Or not." He raised his hands in surrender. "Southlake's good too. Or maybe you want to be on the other side of the city?"

I lifted my left hand. "No ring. We can't be newlyweds." Thank the Fates.

"Okay, just dating."

"Brother and sister," I said, voice assertive. "Our mother is moving to Arlington, and we need to find her a small, affordable house."

"Well, that's no fun," Rupert said.

"It doesn't even matter," I said. "We just need an excuse to get him to open that door. It's not like we're going to spend the day looking for a house."

"Fine," Rupert said, taking his first step into the office. "But I was right, wasn't I? Flower Mound for the kids?"

I elbowed him in the stomach.

Michael's secretary told us to wait on the couch. Two minutes later, Molly walked out, looking blissfully happy, and Michael called us into the office.

I exchanged a panicked look with Rupert. We needed them together so we could time the Kiss precisely.

"I hope we didn't rush you," Rupert said to Molly.

She looked startled to be spoken to. "No, Mikey needs to work. I'll wait here for him."

The secretary huffed and jerked a filing cabinet open.

"We won't take long," I said, walking into the office with Rupert.

I was worried Molly would leave before we finished until Michael promised her he wouldn't take long.

Rupert threw the plan away before we even sat down. "My girlfriend and I are looking to buy a condo." He wrapped his fingers around my hand and pulled me to him. "Isn't that right, schnookums?"

"Mmmhmm." I dug my nails into his hand until he let go.

"I assume you two have already been approved?"

"Well, no," I said.

"But I assure you, money isn't a problem." Rupert puffed up his chest.

"Ah." Michael rose from his seat. "I'm afraid I can't help you find a home until you've been approved. We aren't a brokerage."

"I told you," I said to Rupert.

"Come back as soon as you've been approved, and we'll get you that condo." Michael extended his hand to Rupert.

While Rupert shook his hand, I was already at the door,

doing a little bobby pin magic to make sure the door wouldn't shut all the way. "Coming?" I asked Rupert when the job was done.

He dropped Michael's hand. "Yes, pudding."

We walked just of sight of Michael, Molly, and his secretary then I cast a Veil broad enough to encompass Rupert. As soon as we were invisible to everyone but each other, I started in on him. "We were supposed to be finding a house for our elderly mother."

"You said it yourself, we weren't actually going to look at houses. So what was the harm?"

The harm was that in those few moments, I'd imagined the condo Rupert and I would live in together. It would have huge windows that looked over the city and a huge kitchen, great for hosting parties. Rupert would be great at hosting parties.

"Let's go." I pulled him along by his sleeve.

By the time we'd rounded the corner, Molly was already in the office, and Michael was standing at the door, trying and failing to close it. On one of his opening swings, I flew inside, Rupert waited for the second swing. He'd made it in, but just barely. The door hit his foot and popped back at Michael.

Since I'd gotten there first, I claimed Molly. She was sitting with one leg crossed over the other, swiping through her phone.

"Ready?" I asked Rupert. He was dodging the door, trying to stay as close to Michael as possible. I hoped it would smack him in the face.

"On three."

I nodded and hovered over Molly. "One, two."

Rupert said, "three," and we went in, holding the Kiss for only a second. But it was long enough.

The cord, which had gone invisible after just a few minutes after the Kiss had been Sealed, reappeared. And then it burst at the center, unraveling and sputtering out until the pink and blue sparks fizzled out altogether.

Molly blinked and sat straight up in her chair. Her eyes moved to Michael who was shaking his head. At the same moment, they looked at each other—not like strangers, but like they'd finally taken their sunglasses off and were able to see more clearly. Molly looked down at her phone at the same moment Michael glanced at the clock on the wall.

"I have an appointment in five minutes," Michael said just as Molly said, "I forgot I had plans."

They smiled at each other, lips tight. Molly stood, looking at her phone with great interest. She stopped in front of Michael and looked up from her phone long enough to give him a little wave. He went in for an awkward kiss, which she rejected, giving him her cheek.

I followed Molly out, and Rupert flew close behind me.

We hadn't even made it outside when Molly had someone on the phone. "I thought you were supposed to be my friend," she said to whoever was on the other line. "How could you let me date someone so old?"

"Who's next?" Rupert asked.

"Carmen," I said, pushing off the concrete to get good air. "Hopefully she's working, and hopefully her man is with her."

♥

We weren't so lucky. Carmen was working, but the man she'd been wrongly Fated to wasn't conveniently at her side. Nor did I know where he worked. Or where he lived. Or his name.

Right away, I'd given up, deciding it would be easier to wait until she got off work, hoping she'd go straight to her new lover.

Rupert wasn't as easily discouraged, however. He unVeiled himself and requested a straight razor shave. Carmen didn't have any other customers, so Rupert was in the chair in less than a minute, slathered with shaving crème.

I stayed Veiled, hovering around them, watching each of Carmen's careful swipes.

Rupert hardly had to even try. Carmen gave up information left and right about her man. Jose worked as a car salesman a few miles down the road. I would have been able to find him on name alone, but Carmen went into great detail about his honey-colored eyes and perfect goatee.

As soon as I had what I needed, I flew to the dealership and found my target. Ten minutes after arriving, Rupert called me. He was Veiled and back in the salon, ready to pucker up.

On three, we performed the unSealing Kiss, and I watched their chord dissipate into nothing. Like with Michael and Molly, Jose blinked and tossed off what must be a strange sensation. Unlike Michael and Molly, I was unable to see their relationship end. The cord was proof that it had in fact ended, but there were no outward signs of relief.

"She acting any different?" I asked Rupert through the phone.

"No," he said. "But I don't know why she would. She isn't with Jose."

"You're right," I said, starting to float away.

Just before I'd completely left Jose's side, one of his co-workers walked up to him asking, "Have you screwed up yet? Only a matter of time before that hot thing realizes she's too good for you." His tone was playful, and he punched Jose in the arm.

"Nah, man," Jose said. "I don't know why, but I think she's really into me."

My heart sank. By the time tomorrow came to a close, Carmen would be happily in love with Michael, but Jose would still be alone.

Since Rupert was still in the area, he performed the Kiss on Carmen and Michael. I shoved down my jealousy. I wanted to be the one to give them their happily ever after. But we were in a time crunch, so I gave into his reason. He promised not to mess anything up. When I told him his promises meant nothing to me, he reminded me that his neck was on the line as well. Because his polo shirts would look ridiculous without a neck, I knew he'd take the job seriously.

♥

Jenny and Tyler were a cinch. They were at Jenny's house, trying to decide what to watch on TV. It was obvious that Jenny didn't want to be watching TV at all, but she wanted to do what would make Tyler happy. He was oblivious to her lack of interest but had meandered into the romance category, hoping she'd pick something she liked.

I knew Jenny better than Tyler did. I'd seen her sitting on her sofa late at night. If the TV was on, which it usually wasn't, she watched Family Feud reruns while she did her laundry.

"Let's put them out of their misery," I told Rupert.

He gave me a salute and lowered himself next to Jenny on the couch. "This chick is way too hot for a kid like him."

I couldn't help but smile. Jenny was beautiful, no question, but she was not someone I would have thought Rupert would have categorized as hot. Cute, definitely, but not hot. She wore hardly any makeup, and her clothes were for function, not for getting male attention.

Then Rupert ruined my good impression of him by saying, "Good girls are always hiding some really freaky kinks."

"On three." A puff of air blew my bangs out. "One, two, three," I said quickly.

And just like that, Jenny and Tyler were no more. She stood up and told him point blank, "This isn't going to work."

While Tyler was walking to his car, an old beat-up Ford, I Kissed him, this time for Molly.

"Should you have done that?" Rupert asked.

"We have to reKiss them anyways," I reasoned.

"Yeah, but we don't know where Molly is."

He was right, and I hated him for it.

"I know where she lives," I said,

An hour later, I was at Molly's mansion, and so was her car. I let out a relieved breath. If she wasn't home, I had no idea where to find her.

She was locked in her house, and like last time, there was no way in. We didn't have all day to lounge by the pool, waiting for her to come outside like I had last week, so I decided to be more active.

"UnVeil yourself and ring the doorbell," I said.

"And do what?"

"I don't know. Sell her something."

Rupert rolled his eyes, ready to argue, but I was already flying to the door. I pressed the doorbell, and Rupert flew over, unVeiled.

"I don't have anything to sell," Rupert said. But he straightened his collar and slapped on a devastating smile.

Molly swung the door open. "I don't want anything," she said. Then she got a good look at Rupert. Her posture changed. Instead of an irritated girl ready to slam the door in a stranger's face, she stepped onto the porch, hands folded in front of her with one foot pointed behind her. "Sorry, I'm just used to weirdos trying to sell me stuff."

I went in for the Kiss as soon as she stopped talking.

"I was hoping to borrow your phone," Rupert said.

But suddenly, Molly wasn't interested in Rupert anymore.

The Kiss did exactly what I'd wanted it to. As soon as the pink sparks flew off her lips, blinders fell over her eyes. She wouldn't notice another guy until she was face to face with Tyler. Not even Rupert.

I tugged Rupert's collar.

"I'll just be going then," he said.

Molly closed the door on his face before he'd finished his sentence.

Chapter Twenty-Eight

$\mathscr{I}$ was hungry, so I told Rupert I was taking a lunch break.

"Where do you want to go?" he asked, "I know a great little place close to the club."

"Great," I said. "You go there, and I'll meet you at the club at 1:30."

"Freya," he said, pleading with me.

"I might have to work with you, Rupert. But I do not have to eat my meals with you. 1:30." I popped out of our shared Veil and into my own. Rupert wouldn't be able to see where I went.

As much as I didn't want to eat with Rupert, I didn't want to eat alone. My mind was too miserable of a place to be by myself. So instead of sitting at a booth all by my lonesome, I went to a bar that served appetizers and started a conversation with the bartender.

And I couldn't help myself, as soon as I learned she was single, I told her about Jose. "He works as a car salesman a few miles away."

She shook her head. "Car salesmen are skeezy."

"Not this one," I promised her. "You should at least go for a test drive and see if you like him."

The nachos I'd been eating suddenly tasted awful. I'd just accidentally given this sweet girl advice that sounded a lot like Rupert's words.

I paid my tab and left the bar without finishing my meal. Even without Rupert next to me, I couldn't get away from him.

♥

I arrived at the club before Rupert. I sent him a text saying I was going in early to make sure Norma and this mysterious guy were both there.

Not only was Norma there with Jack, I learned was his name, but so was Tom. He was snuggled up in a booth at the club's restaurant with Susan, Norma's friend.

"This is going to be ugly," I said to myself.

"Really ugly," Rupert said, causing me to jump back. I'd left my Veil visible to other Pavers but hadn't heard Rupert fly next to me."

"At least they're all in the same place," I said.

"How do you want to do this?" Rupert rested his elbow on my shoulder.

I flew out of his reach. "Break the bond between Norma and Jack, then Tom and Susan. As soon as we're clear, I'll Kiss Tom then Norma."

"We better do it fast," Rupert said. "I don't like that there are witnesses."

I nodded, flying to Norma.

Rupert walked over to Jack.

I had to look away. I liked that Rupert walked, and I liked the way he walked.

On three, we unSealed the Kiss between Norma and Jack. Norma took one look at Tom's arm around Susan, and she called her friend a hussy. Susan's mouth was puckered in outrage when Rupert reached her. One, two, three, and I Kissed Tom as Rupert Kissed Susan. Tom's arm fell from around her, and his eyes found Norma's instantly. They'd been sitting next to each other, so I hovered over the table, Kissed Tom again and scooted to Norma, Kissing her too.

They didn't even speak to each other. The Kiss worked fast, drawing them together. Norma pulled Tom's head to hers, and I flew out of the way. They were straight up making out right in front of everyone.

❤

Ivan and the girl he'd been wrongly Fated to were the

hardest to find. They weren't at his house, and since I didn't know who she was or where she lived, we tried his work next. He managed a hole-in-the-wall restaurant Farmer's Branch, where one of the waitresses was more than happy to tell me that he'd given virtually no warning before he'd taken the week off. Before I'd left, she asked me to tell him that two servers called in sick and a fry cook walked out mid-shift, just in case I found him before he bothered to check his messages.

"We should call Daphne," Rupert said as soon as we were airborne. He pulled out his phone.

I was tempted to knock it out of his hand. We'd see if his fancy phone case could withstand a thirty-foot drop. "No," I said, even though he was right.

Daphne would be able to access the name of the girl he'd been Kissed with, but I didn't want to have to ask for her help. I hadn't forgotten what she'd said about "those Darling girls."

"Then should I start knocking on doors?"

"No."

"Freya, you gotta work with me here."

"He's right," a new voice said. I looked to my left and saw Shanae flying beside me. "You only have a day and a half left."

"How long have you been here?" I asked, speeding up.

"Long enough to catch you doing off-the-clock-Cupiding."

"It wasn't Cupiding. It was match-making."

"That's the type of distraction that got you into this mess in the first place."

"No," I said. "Someone is trying to sabotage me. That's what got me into this mess." I shot a look at Rupert, who was typing on his phone. There was that itch to slap his phone out of his hand again. "Are you guys even investigating to find out who did it?" I asked.

"That's none of your concern."

"None of my concern?"

"I suggest you hurry," Shanae said. "Ivan Rodriguez and Nazi Patel have an appointment at the Carrolton Courthouse at 3:30. To get married," she added just before she blinked out.

❤

Never, and I mean never, did I imagine myself stopping a wedding. But that's exactly what I showed up at the courthouse to do.

Nazi was dressed in an adorable white dress with little ruffles on the hem. Ivan wore the cutest darn bow-tie I'd ever seen. They sat in plastic chairs, holding hands.

"I can't believe this is real life," I said, not knowing the words actually came out of my mouth until Rupert slipped his hand in mine.

For just a moment—a teeny, tiny moment of weakness—I squeezed his hand back.

And then I shoved at him. "Let's get it over with."

"Shanae," Rupert said, "if you're still here, now would be a great time to show up."

"Why?" I asked him.

He turned sensitive eyes on me, no hint of his forced charm or lady-killer smile. "She can do this for you. I know it kills you, Freya."

"I told you not to use my name." But I did wait a minute, in case Shanae would show up. But she didn't.

"On three?" Rupert asked.

I nodded, taking a step toward Nazi. At the last second, I shook my head and scooted to Ivan. "He'll at least have a happy ending when this is all over."

"She will too," Rupert said. "Even if I have to make it happen myself."

I wiped away a tear as I knelt before Ivan. "One," I said.

"Two," Rupert said.

"I can't believe how lucky I am," Nazi said.

"Three." I tasted my own tear on Ivan's lips when I pressed my mouth to his.

The cord seemed to take forever to fizzle out, but I knew it hadn't taken any longer than the rest.

"My mom is going to be so excited," Nazi said, smiling at Ivan.

I wished that I could throw a Veil over them so I wouldn't be able to see what came next.

Ivan pulled his hand from Nazi's. "I'm so sorry," he said.

Rupert caught me as I buckled over.

Chapter Twenty-Nine

There was no way I could keep going. Rupert knew it without me having to tell him.

He led me out of the courthouse and deposited me on a bench outside. He sat with me until Lana showed up, taking custody of my broken heart.

It seemed like all the matches I'd made hadn't even counted. Not when I saw the pain in Nazi's eyes. I existed to create love, not break it.

"I mean it," Rupert said, sitting next to me. "I'll make sure she gets her happy ending."

"But her heart is breaking now." I clutched my own heart. For the past week, it had been taking hit after hit, cracking and fracturing with every disappointment. I'd managed to put band-aids on it, holding it together as long as I could, but it had all been temporary. Any other day, I would have taken Nazi's heartbreak hard, today it had been the blow to my chest that split my heart wide open.

"It will heal," Rupert said, and for a moment, I'd forgotten that we were talking about Nazi's heart and not mine. But when I looked up into Rupert's eyes—so open and boring straight into mine—I realized that he was talking about mine too. His brows knit together like he was hurting too. "I'm so sorry."

Could this be real? Could this be a genuine apology from Rupert?

And could I forgive him? We had never been together. He never owed me his loyalty. Had I been too hard on him? I never really believed he was the one sabotaging my Kisses, I'd just wanted it to be him so I could go on hating him. Because without hate, the only thing I had left for him was love.

"I know I hurt you, real bad," Rupert said. "I know it's true." He knelt in front of me, bringing my hands into his. "But baby, you gotta believe me when I say, I helpless without you."

I threw his hands in his face. "That is from *Grease*!" I was so mad, I'd stood from the bench. "You can't even apologize for real. You have to go and make a joke of it, quoting a song."

"From a movie you love," he said, standing too.

"I can't believe I almost believed you were serious."

"I was serious. I am serious."

I laughed. "And for the record," I said, "my heart isn't broken because of you." I spat the words at him, aiming for his stupid pride.

"What?"

"You really think I'm all sad Freya because of you?" I laughed. "You're wrong. It has nothing to do with you."

Moments like these were why I wore heels. There was nothing more satisfying than the sound of my pissed off heels stamping on the concrete as I left Rupert sputtering behind me.

Lana, Penny, and Percy appeared, startling me and ruining my dramatic exit. The looks on their faces couldn't have been more different from each other. Percy looked impressed, even going so far as giving me a slow clap. Penny was all sympathy, rushing toward me with arms wide open to fall into. Lana looked torn. She was trapped somewhere between angry and sad, but when her eyes flitted to Rupert, her face fell in devastation.

"Oh, Freya," she said. "What did you do?" And then she walked passed me, heading right to Rupert.

"Let's go," Penny said, throwing a Veil over both of us. "Coming?" she asked Percy.

"I have to Lana-sit." He tossed an arm in her direction.

I refused to look. Refused to watch my best friend comforting the person I hated most in the world. And refused to let myself see him.

♥

Lana and Percy showed up at my apartment half-way through Bridget Jones Diary.

"I thought I locked it," I said, not even bothering to look at her.

"I used my key."

I turned the volume up.

She flew in front of the TV, blocking my view. "I don't get you," Lana said. "He was being real. Telling you he was sorry. And then you went and let him think it was some other guy. A human guy, who is Fated to be with someone else. Who you never had even the slightest chance of running off into the sunset with."

"Lana," Penny said.

"Don't make me the bad guy, Penny. I'm the only one left who has their mind still inside their head."

"Hey." Percy threw a ball at Lana. "I still have my head."

"My favorite part is coming. Either wait or leave."

That was the wrong thing to say. Lana flew straight to the DVD player and turned the movie off. "You are just scared," Lana said.

"Am not."

"Then explain to me why you superglued yourself to that human's side—"

"His name is Adam."

"That human's side, the moment we all told you Rupert was serious about you. And then, when things got the slightest bit hard with Rupert, you went out and actually met that guy. And after you saw him kiss Jacqueline, you went straight to that dude's house and spent the afternoon with him. You know nothing real can happen between you. But its easier to stay in your little fantasy world than to let yourself feel something real. If you want your sunshine and rainbows ending, Freya, you have to deal with the thunderstorms."

Chapter Thirty

$\mathcal{R}$upert wasn't waiting at my door the next morning. And he hadn't left me even one text message telling me where to meet him.

Lana, who'd slept on my couch—refusing to leave even though I told her I didn't want her in my apartment—was playing middleman. And so were Percy and Penny, because I was refusing to speak directly to her. If she wanted a thunderstorm, I'd give her one.

After the most awkward morning in my life—Penny tip-toeing around my feelings, Lana disregarding them completely, and Percy trying, for once, to stay as far from the drama as he could—I met Rupert in front of Cupid HQ.

No bouquet of roses. No apology letters. No bad pick-up lines. Rupert was a shell. And I'd made him that way.

Irritatingly, it didn't make me feel any better.

"Should we unSeal the last couple then go back to yesterday's couples and force them to Seal their Kisses?"

"Not yet," I said. It was stupid, I wasn't going to be able to avoid seeing Adam and Andie together again, but I didn't think my heart could take it if we showed up at his house to find them entwined in bed together. "Let's start with Ivan and Jenny. We never reKissed them."

"I did it."

"When?"

"Last night. Lana came with me."

I laughed, but it wasn't sincere. "Of course y'all did."

"What's that supposed to mean?"

"Nothing." I shook my head. "I guess I should say thanks."

"No." Rupert shook his head. "There's nothing like that going on between Lana and me."

That surprised me enough to look at him. "I know that." As mad as I was by her, and as betrayed as I'd felt that she'd taken his side over mine, I hadn't thought even for a second that something was going on between them.

"Good," Rupert said, pulling the folded list of names and a pen out of his pocket. Were those the same pants he'd been wearing yesterday?

They were. And he had on the same shirt too.

"Norma and Tom Sealed their Kiss on the spot." Rupert crossed their names off the list. "I didn't see Jenny and Ivan Seal the Kiss, but as soon as I Kissed her, she called her friend and said she wanted to go out, so I'd put money on the fact that they're at least half-way there, if not Sealed already."

I was about to say we should start with them, but Rupert was still talking.

"Molly and Tyler were at the same house party. When I left them, they were sucking face. That Kiss is Sealed." He crossed their names off his list.

"You guys went back to Tyler and Molly?" I asked. "It didn't seem like Lana was gone that long." Or maybe she hadn't stayed on my couch all night like I'd thought.

"No," Rupert said, "I, uh, couldn't sleep, so I checked in with all the couples. Carmen and Michael met, but they haven't Sealed the Kiss yet. They made plans for lunch, so they'll probably Seal it then."

"You worked all night?"

Rupert shrugged. "I couldn't relax."

"Jacqueline would have been happy to help you relax." I regretted the words as soon as they'd left my mouth. "Sorry," I said, wincing. "I shouldn't have said that."

"I'm not interested in Jacqueline." The sentence was simple, but it carried so much weight. "Or Daphne, or Mariah, or anyone else."

I shook my head. "I said I was sorry." I snatched the paper from his hands. The only two names not crossed off were Carrie Timms and Adam Hannon.

"I went to see them, too," Rupert said.

"Who? Them?" I held the paper up. "Why? You need another Cupid to break the Seal."

"Because I wanted to know."

My throat went dry. "Know what?"

"What he has," Rupert said. "That I don't."

I couldn't look at him. My eyes stayed glued to Adam's name written in Rupert's perfect handwriting.

"He seems pretty great. You were right. Burly."

"Rupert."

"He cooks, too." Rupert's laugh was cold. "Doesn't seem right that a guy can build a house and make Tuscan Stuffed Chicken."

"Rupert," I said again.

He cleared his throat. "And she, that girl he was making it for, is a total nightmare."

"Andie was there?" Of course she was.

"She's a real piece of work. I mean, the man slaved over a hot stove all night, and she still found ways to criticize him."

"You should have seen her before she was Sealed with him. She made Tessa look like a happy camper," I said, referring to the biggest whiner we knew.

Rupert laughed, a real one, but then it fizzled out. "The other girl, Carrie, looks like she's perfect for him," Rupert said, then hurried to continue, "And I don't mean that to be mean, Frey. Fates, you could make that man so happy, but—"

"But I'm not Fated to him," I said. *Because I'm Fated to you.*

"Yeah." He looked awkwardly at his hands. "But there has to be some peace in knowing that since he can't be with you, he'll be with someone who deserves him."

I nodded through a lump in my throat. I didn't know if the building tears were caused by the image I'd conjured of Adam and Carrie living the rest of their lives together or if they were caused by the pain I knew Rupert was holding back. Because it was so obvious.

"Then I guess we should get to it, huh?" I folded the list back into its neat square and handed it to Rupert. "Let's go give them a happy ending."

♥

We went to Carrie's first.

She was in her room, alone. She was doing her makeup though, a promising sign that she was going somewhere other than work because she hadn't been wearing makeup when I'd seen her at the shop before.

She wasn't wearing a sign telling us of her plans though, so Rupert and I had to wait out the morning, hoping she'd take us to her guy. We hovered around her window in the thickest cloud of polite silence ever in the history of the world. We took turns asking about each others' families—his parents were doing well, and my sisters and parents were fine.

He asked me if I'd been to the sandwich shop around the corner—I had, it was great—and I asked him if he'd tried the pizza joint down the road—he hadn't, but would keep it in mind next time he was in the area at lunchtime. I was about to ask him if he'd been to the juice bar off the square when Carrie walked out the front door.

Eager to be one step closer to getting the day over with so I could crawl back to bed and sleep off my two-week suspension, I darted after Carrie, ready to follow her car wherever it was going.

I sank to the pavement when I saw that she was heading to the furniture store. I would go crazy if I had to wait out her workday with Rupert.

"I know where the guy lives," I said. "I can see if he's there and we can unSeal the Kiss on the phone like we did for Carmen and Jose."

Rupert said, "Okay," just as Carrie's got out of her car. But she didn't walk into her shop. She walked to doors past it, and into a coffee shop.

Rupert and I tried to see inside as we hung outside of the door, waiting for someone to open it. Carrie went right to a table instead of waiting in line. A moment later, the door swung open, and the guy she'd been Sealed to walked into the coffee shop.

As soon as Carrie saw him, her eyes lit up, and she stood from her chair. He went right to her and pulled her into his arms, planting a kiss right on her lips. "I missed you," he said and slid his hand into hers.

"I missed you too." She gave him another kiss. "I didn't know if you wanted to drink the coffee here or get it to go, so I thought I'd wait for you," she said.

He looked to the ceiling like he was weighing both options. "How long until you have to be at the store?" he asked.

"Not till ten."

"Then let's have a cup here, then take one to go."

"That's what I was hoping you'd say."

They had the entire conversation with their faces only inches from each other's, so Rupert and I had to wait until they walked toward the line to unSeal the Kiss.

"Ready?" he asked.

"Yeah."

We'd done it so many times in the past twenty-four hours, we didn't even bother counting down. We nodded at each other, and I pressed my lips to Carrie's at the exact moment Rupert's touched the man she was about to fall out of love with.

The cord dissolved, but their hands didn't leave each others. She even leaned her head on his shoulder.

"What are you going to get?" she asked him.

"Whatever you're having," he said.

"Let's go," Rupert said, touching my shoulder.

"He's never going to find someone as great as her," I said, letting him lead me out of the coffee shop.

"You don't know that," Rupert said. "I think he might be Nazi's type."

I knew he was wrong, Ivan was nothing like this guy, but I liked that he was still thinking of her, so I kept my thought to myself.

Chapter Thirty-One

There was a shiny, red Volkswagen Beatle sitting in Adam's driveway.

This would make our job easier, but it didn't mean I liked the implication. Andie had stayed over.

"He leaves the back door open for Ruby," I said when Rupert flew to a window.

"He does that all the time? I just thought I got lucky last night."

"Yeah," I said, not moving an inch toward the backyard.

"Maybe I could call Daphne and see if she'll come help with this one?"

That got my wings going. "No."

Rupert raised his hands in the universal don't shoot gesture.

I soared past him but slowed as Ruby barreled out the back door, barking like crazy as soon as she smelled us. I was surprised she hadn't smelled Rupert and his cologne when we were still in the front.

I didn't even think about my dress as I landed on my knees on the grass. Ruby stopped barking as soon as she singled out my scent. Her tail propelled her straight toward me, and even though she couldn't see me, her aim was perfect when she jumped on me, covering my face in wet, welcoming kisses. I buried my face in her neck, pulling her as close to me as possible. Saying goodbye to her would be as hard as saying goodbye to Adam.

"I'll go, uh, see what's going on inside," Rupert said.

I nodded but didn't trust myself to answer verbally. The tears were already falling down my cheeks, being kissed away by Ruby's tongue. If I had to speak, I'd fall apart.

Ruby was on her back, enjoying an invisible tummy scratch when Rupert came back outside. "They're eating breakfast," he said.

It could have been my breakfast. It had been so close to being my breakfast.

"There's nothing else left to do, is there?"

He shook his head. "How do you want to do it?" He cleared his throat. "I mean, would it be easier if I—"

"No." I shook my head, not meeting his eyes. "I want to."

Rupert nodded, and I followed him through the back door, Ruby trailing behind me.

"Why did she let you in the house?" I asked. I was stalling, and I knew Rupert knew it, but it was a valid question. She'd chased Penny away.

"I smell like you," Rupert said. "She was all teeth last night until she tackled me and got her nose close to my chest. She sniffed the spot like crazy and started whining. I think she knew I wasn't you, but I guess she trusted that if you let me close enough for your scent to wear off, then I wasn't all bad."

"Smart girl." I gave her a pat on the head.

Andie wrinkled her nose as she watched Adam pour syrup onto his pancakes.

"I'll admit," I said, getting closer to Adam, but still not letting myself get a good look at him. "I'm looking forward to the moment he kicks her out of the house."

Rupert laughed. "I hope he tells her off."

And then there was nothing left to do but break the Seal. I let my eyes fall on his face, taking him in one last time before he'd forever belong to Carrie. I memorized the planes of his cheekbones and the six freckles on the right side of his face. He was handsome, absolutely no doubt about it, but I must have come to accept our fate apart because the pull that had at one time forced me toward him was no longer there. He was just a boy meant to love a girl. Who wasn't me.

I leaned in, knowing somehow, that Rupert would time his Kiss with mine.

There was a drop of syrup on Adam's lip, and I focused on it as I brought my lips to his. I leaned into the Kiss too much, it wouldn't feel like a whisper on his mouth like it was supposed to, it would feel like a kiss. A kiss he couldn't see.

When I pulled away, I liked the syrup from my lip as I watched the knot that joined Adam and Andie untie and then the fizzle of the cord, until the blue sparks disappeared on Adam's lips.

He held his hand to his mouth gently, looking right at me but not seeing me.

"How can you eat those?" Andie asked. "You put half a bottle of syrup on them."

Adam breathed in deeply and closed his eyes, fingers tightening on the fork in his hand. Finally, he dropped it, and it clattered onto his plate. "Why does it matter how I eat my pancakes?"

"Because," she said, putting her own fork down. "You aren't always going to have a job that burns so many calories. I'm not trying to be with a guy who gets fat when he gets a desk job because he's not used to watching his caloric intake."

"Who says I'm getting a desk job?"

She scoffed. "You aren't actually planning to cut scrap wood all your life, are you?"

"Scrap wood?"

I thought I would enjoy this part, watching them fall out of fake love, but I was too tired of watching people's lives fall apart. I knew this was only temporarily, within twenty-four hours, Adam will be so wrapped up with Carrie that he'll forget there was ever an Andie, but I still couldn't watch it.

I walked out the back door to wait the fight out with Ruby. She followed me like I'd hoped she would, and I picked up the knotted rope and tossed it into the grass. She ran after it, tail wagging as she retrieved it and brought it to me. She searched for my hand trying to put it right in my grasp, and when she couldn't find it, she whined and dropped it by my feet.

I looked back at the house. Rupert's back took up most of the doorframe. His shoulders were shaking as he laughed at the raised voices in the kitchen. Judging by the sound, Adam was finally giving her his true opinion of her. Feeling safe, at least for a moment, I untethered myself from the Veil Rupert had us both in.

As soon as Ruby saw me, she jumped up, dropping the rope in her excitement. Her ears flew against her head as she sprinted toward me, her whole body wagging in excitement when she reached my outstretched hands.

She knocked me to my back, kissing me and barking in excitement. I tried to push her off without pushing her away, but every time I got back to my knees, she pushed me over again.

"She missed you."

I froze. Adam was standing on his patio, laughing, one arm on the doorframe, the other on his hip.

"I'm so sorry," I said, looking around for an excuse. Maybe I'd find one in the tree or on the grass. "I was just at my friends around the corner again, and I wanted to say hi to Ruby, but I saw the car, so I didn't think I should knock."

"Don't be sorry." Adam shook his head, walking into the grass. "I'm glad you came." He shoved his hands in his pockets. "Look, about the other day."

I waved my hands. "Don't worry about it. I get it, more than you know."

"It's done." He scratched his jawline. "Whatever 'it' was. It's very over."

"I'm sorry to hear that."

He scrunched up his face like he was trying to decide on something. "This probably sounds awful, and I know I don't deserve another chance, but do you think we could maybe try for that date?"

"Oh, I don't—"

"I really have no idea what came over me with Andie. She's, like, everything I wouldn't want in a girlfriend—"

"But when you saw her again, the stars seemed to align, and you suddenly saw her in a new light?"

"Yeah." He laughed, scratching his chin again. "But then, just now, I saw her again, really saw her, and it was like the spell she'd put on me broke or something." He took a step closer. "And its crazy, because as soon as she left, here you are."

"Here I am," I said, and I took a step toward him.

Where had all my earlier resolve gone? Before, in the

kitchen, I'd said goodbye to him with that kiss, really meant it. And I'd walked away, outside with Ruby, knowing that the next time I Kissed him, it would be to send him to Carrie. But now, with Andie gone, and without being able to see Rupert, it was like Adam and I were the only two people on this earth, and I couldn't imagine walking away from him now.

He took another step, and I covered the last bit of grass between us. Ruby nudged my hand with the rope, but I couldn't even drag my eyes off Adam long enough to toss it for her.

"It's like fate keeps shoving us together," Adam said, reaching for the side of my face.

It felt exactly like Fate.

Like Destiny.

Like a Cupid's Kiss.

I backed up, letting Adam's hand fall from my cheek. And I kept backing up, despite the magnetic pull that drew me closer to him.

He followed me like he was drawn to me as well. "I didn't mean to push you," he said. He walked passed Ruby who was begging him to throw the rope.

I kept walking, trying my hardest to turn my back on him, but I couldn't convince my body to do it.

"Did I scare you?"

"No," I said, tripping over an uneven spot in the grass. "I just can't."

"Can't what? I know I screwed up with Andie, but I promise, that was … it was …"

"A mistake, I know." I'd stopped walking, even though I was screaming at my feet to go, to move, to run. I wasn't in control of my body. The same way I hadn't been in control of it the first time I'd seen Adam.

The pull had been strong then, so strong that I hadn't been in control of my wings when they flew me toward him. But it had been strong enough to fight. I hadn't known him then, so the pull was similar to when any Fated couple was first Kissed.

The need to be near them was strong, but it hadn't sent them straight into each other's arms. But with couples who'd gotten the chance to know each other, like Tom and Norma and Glen and Ana, couples who had real feelings for each other, the Kiss practically Sealed itself. Like it was trying to do now.

The more I used my mind, the more I was able to keep the pull at bay. I took another step back as he'd closed the distance again.

Think, Freya, think.

How did this happen? There I was, playing with Ruby, Adam and Andie were inside breaking up while Rupert watched.

I took another step backward.

Rupert. He'd done this. He'd Kissed Adam and me.

My back hit the fence.

But why? Why had he done it?

The answer was there, right at the edge of my mind, but I couldn't grasp it.

I closed my eyes, and using the fence as my guide, I turned and walked away.

"You're leaving?" Adam asked. "You can't go, Freya. Please. Give me a chance. I'll do anything."

My outstretched hand found the gate, and I tugged it open, finally opening my eyes when I was on the other side. I pulled it closed behind me. Then I was running.

"Freya!" he called, and I heard him open the gate. Ruby barked.

I kept running. I ran right out of my heels and kept going until I'd put two houses between us. Then I cut between the third and fourth house, and as soon as I knew I was out of his view, I threw up my Veil and pushed off the ground, soaring into the air.

Adam's run slowed when he spotted my shoe on the sidewalk. He bent down and picked it up, tapping it against his leg. Ruby ran past him until she reached my other shoe. She picked it up, looking around like I'd pop out of the bushes, and we'd play this new version of fetch again.

I held onto a telephone pole, half to keep myself balanced, half to anchor myself so I wouldn't go back to Adam.

With sagging shoulders, Adam called Ruby to come back and tried to grab the shoe from her mouth. She avoided his hand and trotted past him, straight to through the gate. Tail low, she brought my pump to the corner of the backyard and placed it on top of a pile of treasures between her dog house and the fence.

I couldn't convince myself to fly away until Adam was in his house.

And only when I was out of Denton could I grasp the thought that had been on the edge of my mind.

Rupert had Kissed Adam and me for the same reason I'd come to terms with Kissing Adam and Carrie. Because *there has to be some peace in knowing that since he can't be with you, he'll be with someone who deserves him.*

Rupert had taken his own advice. If he couldn't be with me, I'd at least be with someone I deserved.

But Rupert had it all wrong.

Chapter Thirty-Two

$\mathscr{I}$ made it to Michael's office in time to follow his car to the restaurant where he was meeting Carmen.

Still not trusting myself enough to not fly back to Adam, I unVeiled myself and decided to watch their lunch in the flesh. That, of course, required a pit-stop at a gas station where I bought a pair of Corona Lite flip-flops, earning a confused look from the cashier. It probably wasn't every day that he saw a woman in a polka-dot skirt walk into his store barefoot. Then again, gas stations were always the best people watching spots.

I had planned to eat alone, but a surprise guest took the seat across from me while I waited for my Shirley Temple. Not dirty this time.

I'd sent Shanae a message, asking her to meet me here, but I'd expected her to have to travel across the metroplex before she made an appearance. I should have known better.

"I have to admit," she said, putting on her glasses to look at the menu. "I was surprised you asked for me to come."

"No one is more surprised than I am."

"What do you need?" She was always so business oriented, to the point.

I'd hoped to have at least a half an hour at lunch to find the right words to ensure her help without raising any red flags. I took the seconds the waiter was at our table to give me my drink and ask Shanae what she wanted to come up with a plan.

"Exactly what is your role in all of this?" I asked, studying her face.

"I'm an auditor. I audit."

"Yeah. I know that. But like, is your hands—or Kiss—tied?'"

"If you want something, Freya, it would you do good to just ask for it."

"I need you to perform my final Kiss."

Her eyes darted to Michael and Carmen who were sitting on the same side of the booth. The server was standing in front of them, waiting for them to peel their eyes from each other long enough to order their food.

"It looks to me like you don't need my help," Shanae said.

"Not them. Their Kiss will be Sealed before they leave this restaurant."

"Then who? O'Connor-Rodriguez, Wells-Schein, and Keenan-Owens are all done deals. Like you said, these two are as good as Sealed, and I know you and Rupert were on the Hannon-Timms case this morning. What's left?"

"You knew we were on the Hannon-Timms case?"

"Yes." She nodded and accepted her water from the server. She told him we still needed a minute before she said, "I was at the coffee house, and I saw the two of you head to the Hannon house. I checked on the other couples first, and then followed Mendoza here." She pulled off her glasses. "Don't tell me something went wrong with Hannon-Timms. Freya, you only have eleven hours before their Kisses have to be Sealed."

"That's where I was hoping you would help me." I gave her my best smile. "I was hoping you'd do that last little Kiss for me. But um, there's something else." My smile grew plastic. "I also need you to unKiss me."

"UnKiss you?"

I recognized it the moment she flipped her super-Cupid vision on. All supervisorial Cupids could see the link between Fateds at will, but they only resorted to the ability when necessary. They couldn't fly around all day seeing every cord linking every Fated couple.

Her eyes widened, and she shook her head. "Freya. You and I both know I can't overrule Destiny. If you've received Cupid's Kiss, you're stuck with it." She pinched the bridge of her nose. "And frankly, I don't even know why you're fighting this. You and Rupert are made for each other. Forget why," she said, "How are you fighting it? A couple like you and Rupert should have Sealed the Kiss on the spot. Speaking of that, why have you already been—"

I stopped her. "That's the thing. I wasn't Kissed to Rupert."

She shewed the server away with a swift hand motion as soon as she approached our table.

"Impossible."

Fully aware that I wasn't supposed to know I was Fated to Rupert, I leaned forward."

"Why is that impossible?"

Her features went pinched, and she looked around for the server.

"Is Rupert my Fated?" I asked, hoping I'd had the right amount of shock in my tone.

"I can't tell you that."

"I think you just did."

She blew air out of her nose and whispered, "You two were due to be Kissed last week, but something went wrong, and the Kiss didn't get assigned."

She kept talking swiftly. "We figured it out when you two had a very public argument—in which you slapped him—so HQ thought it best to wait until you reconciled before you were Kissed. Even a Destiny can't overrule blind hatred. If you suddenly went goo-goo eyes for someone who made you so clearly unhappy, you'd figure out it was the Kiss forcing you together, and you wouldn't Seal it. That's why he was the one assigned to help you get out of this mess. The Destiny of those five other couples could have been easily rewritten, but Destiny has too big a plan for the two of you. It couldn't be rewritten. You and Rupert were supposed to reconcile your differences promptly so you'd be ready for your Kiss."

"That's why we had a two-day time limit," I said.

"Yes." She spat the word. "And now, you've gone and screwed it up on a level I thought impossible even for you."

"I'm going to chose to take that as a compliment instead of an insult," I said.

"How? It was meant to be insulting."

"Because I still need you to break my Kiss." I pointed to my lips.

"How am I supposed to do that by myself, Freya?"

"I was hoping you'd have an idea."

"Well, I don't."

"Who was the Cupid assigned to Rupert and me? Wouldn't it be in their best interest to have me available for Rupert?"

I knew I was right when she pulled out her phone. A moment later she said, "Daphne, I need your help."

Chapter Thirty-Three

With that one phone call, everything clicked into place.

"When exactly was I scheduled to be Kissed?"

"Saturday."

"Saturday was when my O'Connor-Rodriguez failed. They were so close, Shanae, I mean, seconds from Sealing, and then bam, Ivan just backed out."

"What does that have to do with anything?"

"Two days later, Rupert and I made plans for our first date—real date—no Kiss needed. But before that same day, before the date actually happened, I was Kissed to someone else."

"No." Shanae shook her head.

"Yes. But I didn't Seal that Kiss. I would have, trust me, I wanted to kiss him, you don't even know how close I came to it, but I didn't because I remembered Rupert. The whole week I was a total mess, unable to concentrate on anything but Adam."

"Adam is this person you were Kissed to?"

"Yes."

"I don't know a Cupid named Adam."

"That's because he's not a Cupid. He's a human."

"Oh, Freya." She covered her face with her hands. "This gets worse by the second."

"But," I said, cutting her off before she could lecture me. "I didn't Seal it." I decided it was best not to get into detail about all the ways I'd almost Sealed it. "I didn't know it had happened at the time, but I resisted because I knew how wrong it would have been."

"I don't think you have any idea how wrong."

"Anyways," I continued, "When I showed up at his house today it was different. I wasn't drawn to him the way I'd been before. I still had feelings for him, for sure, but they weren't the same."

"You waited it out. The week went by without Sealing, so you're free. You don't need to break the Seal." Her eyes went foggy again, and I knew she was looking at my cord. "Or, it should be the case."

"That's where it gets a little more complicated." I took a deep breath. "You know that saying, if you love someone, let them go?"

She nodded, but she didn't look happy about it.

"That's what Rupert did. He thought being with Adam would make me happy, so he let me go."

"You mean he broke just about every Cupid rule, and Kissed you to a human?"

"Because he loves me that much."

She groaned. "Idiot."

"Yeah. He is." I smiled. "But, my point to all of this, is that Daphne is the one who Kissed me to Adam the first time. The time that screwed everything up. And she has been covering her tracks by messing up all of my matches so it would look like it was my fault."

"And why would she do that."

"Easy," I shrugged. "She was jealous that I was going to take away her favorite playboy. If I was off the market, better yet, tossed out of the Paver's Cloud, she'd keep Rupert."

"As her colleague, I'd like to tell you that I didn't believe she was capable. But as someone whose boyfriend she slept with, I'm going to say it's true."

"Darius?" I asked, referring to her husband.

"Hell no, I wouldn't marry a cheater no matter what Destiny said. You know Shamus?"

"The guy who's in charge of housing?"

"Yup."

"Darius is a whole flight of steps up from him."

"You don't have to tell me."

"Tell you what?" Daphne asked, walking up to our table.

Shanae gave me a "keep your mouth shut" look before she turned to Daphne, as professional as ever. "How much trouble she'll be in if she doesn't get her matches Sealed before the end of the day."

At the reminder of why we were at this restaurant, not eating, I looked at the table Michael and Carmen shared. Their food was in front of them, but their mouths were too busy smooching to eat.

"That one's done," I said, throwing a twenty on the table.

♥

"I still don't understand why I'm here," Daphne said. "And why are we leaving without eating? I flew all the way down here to join you for lunch."

"I didn't invite you to lunch," Shanae said, "I told you to meet me at the restaurant."

"At lunchtime."

"Not relevant." Shanae waved for us to follow her as she walked to the back of the restaurant. As soon as we were out of view of onlookers, she cast a Veil over all three of us.

"Where are we going?" Daphne asked. "We're busy in the office today. Half the staff has doubles." She gave me a long look. "Covering for slackers."

"I've already told Charlotte to find someone to cover you."

Despite Daphne's many questions, Shanae refused to answer them. She'd put her headphones in, insisting that she flies best while listening to her audiobook. I'd have given almost anything to have a set of headphones myself because Daphne just turned her questions on me. I played dumb, claiming to not know what Shanae was up to.

The pull to be near Adam had never gone away, but with the miles between us, the tug was equal to that first feeling of hunger you get when your body is trying to tell you that food would be needed in your near future. But when I'd crossed the Denton border, the pull grew stronger, like being hungry and smelling a roast simmering in the crockpot. When I got to Adam's street, the pull was like when you'd been starving for hours, and the waiter keeps bringing food to every table but yours. And when I saw Adam's house, the pull was like that deep, hunger that controlled every thought you had, and you found yourself seriously considering eating rocks just to have something to fill the gnawing emptiness.

"Why are we here?" Daphne said, eyes cagey.

"I think you know," Shanae said.

"N-no."

"We're here to undo what you did."

"I didn't do anything."

"We both know that's a lie."

"It isn't."

"Okay then," Shanae said, "I guess I'll have to get Charlotte down here to trace the Kiss so we can get to the bottom of it."

"Don't." Daphne reached out to cover the phone.

Rupert. Rupert. Rupert. I said his name over and over to remind myself of why I shouldn't go to Adam. Why swallowing rocks would only be a temporary fix that would just hurt me worse in the end. Rupert. Rupert. Rupert.

"Then get in that house and help me UnSeal this Kiss."

Daphne went without another word.

"Wait," I called to Daphne.

"Freya, you know she has to do this," Shanae said.

"I know. It's not that." I shrugged out of my cardigan. "You're going to need this to get past Ruby."

Daphne rolled her eyes, but grabbed my cardigan, holding it out from her like it was something vile that would taint her if she held it too closely.

When it was just Shanae and me left hovering above Adam's street, I said, "I can't get closer." Even one more inch would be too far to turn back from.

"I know," Shanae said. "I remember." As she dialed Daphne, she tugged my arm, leading me away from the house. "Are you ready?"

I nodded, then realized she was talking to Daphne, not me.

"One, two, three."

Shanae's lips landed on mine, and I was finally Kissed by a Cupid.

It just wasn't how I'd ever imagined it happening.

Chapter Thirty-Four

$\mathcal{O}$n the flight back to the Paver's Cloud, I tried to make sense of my feelings.

As soon as the Kiss had been unSealed, the unnatural pull to Adam had vanished instantly. But the fondness I had for him was as strong as ever. I no longer felt like I'd be willing to jeopardize my Veil to go to him, but I still felt remorse for the life I could have had with him.

Those feelings were real, and I doubted they were going to evaporate anytime soon, but the closer I got to the Paver's Cloud, the more other feelings filled me.

Like the ones I had for Rupert.

They were complicated, filled with leftover tidbits of betrayal and pain, but the negative was overshadowed by the gratitude and affection I felt toward him.

In the deepest parts of me, I'd known I'd loved Rupert since that first day of Cupid school when he walked past me, tossing me a wink. I'd felt so strongly toward him that I'd felt guilty for feeling that way, like loving Rupert would be a betrayal of my future Fated. How could I look at another boy when there was one made especially for me?

Over the years, I'd grown to think of him as the greatest temptation of my life. Little did I know, he was meant to be the great love of my life.

When I crossed into the Veil of the Paver's Cloud, I started flying faster, heading straight to The Parched Paver to see Rupert. And not because a Kiss was pulling me to him, but because I'd known Rupert my whole life, and I knew where I'd find him.

Also knowing Rupert, I'd fully prepared myself for finding him wrapped up in Jacqueline or Mariah's arms, trying to dumb his feelings with a warm body. I told myself not to let the jealousy take over, to be understanding. I could do that for him. For us.

But when flew in, I saw Jacqueline and her friends sitting at a cocktail table by the dart board, without Rupert. Mariah was sitting with Daryl, stealing a sip from his drink.

Rupert was at the bar next to Lana. She was using her hands, trying to explain something, surely with one great metaphor or another, but he only stared into his Old Fashioned, swirling the amber liquid in his glass.

Lana saw me first. She stopped mid-sentence, arms frozen in the air. Rupert paused, set down his glass, looking up at her. When a knowing smile curved her lips, Rupert turned to see what had caused the change.

He swiveled on his barstool, facing me. For the first time in forever, his expression was unreadable.

I went to him, my heart picking up speed with each step I took closer to him. When I was five feet away, he stood.

Lana put a hand on his shoulder, pushing him back into his seat.

"Did it hurt?" I asked, finally right in front of him. "When you fell from heaven?" It was the worst line I could come up with, and the first he'd ever used on me.

He gave me an exasperated eye-roll, one like I'd given him every time he'd used it on me. "That the best you've got?"

"It worked on me, so I thought I'd give it a shot."

Lana discreetly flew away, leaving Rupert and me alone at the bar.

"How are you here?" he asked, reaching to touch my arm, but then drawing it back. "You're supposed to be down there, with him."

"No," I said, "I'm exactly where I'm supposed to be."

"I don't understand. I Kissed you two. I saw the sparks. It worked."

I laughed. "Oh, it worked all right. But it wasn't real. It was never real. With him. The only person its real with is you. I was too afraid of being hurt to see it before. But I see it now. Rupert, you're the one for me. Always have been."

"She's right," Shanae said, appearing right next to us. "You're the one for her. And now she's ready."

"Is this it?" Rupert looked first to Shanae and then back to me. "Our Kiss?"

Shanae nodded, her smile enormous.

"No," I said, stepping closer to Rupert so she couldn't get between us. "I don't want it."

Hurt flashed onto his face, twisting my heart.

"I want you," I said quickly, pulling his hands around my waist. "But I don't want the Kiss. I want to choose you. I want to live every day knowing you are the choice I made for myself." I rubbed my hand over his chest, feeling his heart thudding. "And I want to know you chose me. That is, if I am the one you chose."

His hands were cupping my face, forcing me to look into his deep brown eyes. I saw his answer in them and thought that was all I needed, but then he said, "Freya, I chose you when I was five years old, and I have made that choice every day. I will continue to choose you for the rest of my life."

I sealed my lips to his as soon as the last word was out.

I'd kissed so many people in my life as a Cupid, but this was the first time I'd been kissed back. And it was better than anything I ever imagined.

Rupert's lips pushed back against mine, sending a shiver down my spine. One of his hands moved from my face to the small of my back, pulling me even closer to him, like our whole bodies were kissing, not just our lips. He buried his fingers into my hair, tilting my head back so he could deepen this kiss.

I was a gooey puddle in Rupert's arms, letting myself drown in him.

I could have stayed there forever, kissing him until our Hundred was over and we were old and gray. But something hit the back of my head. I stilled my lips on Rupert's for just a second, and then realized I didn't care. The building could collapse around us, and I'd still be happy to go on, kissing Rupert. Then something hit the side of my face. And then his.

"Get a room!" Percy yelled, tossing another ball at us.

Rupert kissed me once more, a simple sweet kiss, then he

pressed his lips to my nose, then my cheek, then the other, and finally went back to my mouth.

Shanae cleared her throat.

I could ignore a tsunami, but Shanae, I couldn't ignore. I turned to her, snuggling my head in Rupert's chest as he wrapped his arms around me.

"Please?" I asked, realizing that she hadn't technically approved my request to be with Rupert without Sealing a Kiss.

"Remember what I said." She looked at me long and hard. "You two have a Destiny together that is bigger than the two of you. Bigger than any couple. Don't make me regret this."

And then she blinked out of our site, and I went back to kissing Rupert.

Chapter Thirty-Five

$\mathscr{R}$upert and I had one more thing to do that night before we could put the mess behind us.

All done up in my red dress—Rupert's favorite—I sat next to Carrie at the Silverleaf, sipping my Dirty Shirley and eyeing the room for Adam.

I'd walked into her shop minutes before her store closed and asked her to grab a drink with me. She was surprised at first, which was to be expected. I was her customer, not her friend after all, but after a moment, she shrugged and said she could use a drink.

Rupert's part had been tougher, getting Adam to come out to the bar. I had no idea what he had planned, but he promised he had it under control. I was only a little concerned that his plan had involved Percy.

"You would not believe the weekend I've had," Carrie said, speaking over the music. The bar was between bands, and the room was crowding with more people by the second. Apparently, whoever was headlining tonight, was a crowd favorite.

"Try me," I said, smiling.

Halfway through her story of a whirlwind romance that hadn't even lasted forty-eight hours, Rupert walked in, looking as gorgeous as ever. I tried to keep my attention on Carrie pouring her heart to me, but with Rupert so close, I was having a hard time.

His eyes found mine right away, even though I hadn't told him where we were. For a second, that worried me, made me fear that a Kiss was controlling us, and not our feelings. But when he casually walked passed me, and I was able to keep my eyes on Carrie, I knew I was in control of myself. I may be obsessed with the man, but a Kiss had nothing to do with it.

Five minutes later, Adam walked in, paid the cover charge, and headed right for the bar without seeing me.

Carrie's words dried-up as she saw who I was looking at. "He," she said, "is beautiful." She giggled, covering her mouth with wide eyes. "Listen to me. I was talking about another guy not two minutes ago."

"Hey, you're single. No harm, no foul."

"A guy like that," she said, pointing to him with his beer, "would never look at me twice."

I snapped my head to her. "Why would you say that?"

"You saw him." She tossed her hand in his direction. "And you see me." She waved her hand over herself.

She looked adorable. Her hair sat in a messy bun on top of her head, and curly tendrils fell around her face, framing it perfectly. Her paint-splattered overalls fit her well, showing off her cute figure.

"I think you should go talk to him," I said, nodding. "Yep. Get back on that horse."

"No way," she said, shaking her head.

"Fine, walk up to the bar and get another drink. See if he talks to you."

"No. I don't even need another drink." She held up her glass, showing she still had half her beer left.

I snatched it out of her hand, plugging my nose as I downed the last few gulps of her beer. "Now you need a drink."

Her mouth fell open, and a disbelieving laugh pushed out. "I can't believe you did that."

"Go." I gave her gentle push on the arm.

She took a step forward, turning back to me and shaking her head.

I pushed her in the butt with the toe of my pump.

As soon as I was certain she would follow through, I ran into the bathroom and into a stall, Veiling myself as soon as I had privacy. Leaving the stall closed but not locked, I flew over the top and barely made it through the restroom before the door swung shut. I was hovering beside Adam when Carrie reached the bar top.

Her neck was blotchy, and her hands were stuffed in her pockets as she stood next to Adam, waiting for a bartender to notice her.

Adam's nostrils flared, and he took in a deep breath like he was smelling something familiar. My heart sank, I was too close. The last thing I wanted was for him to be thinking of me when Carrie was standing next to him.

But his nose turned to her, and a smirk slid onto his face. "You smell like wood stain," Adam said. "It happens to be one of my favorite scents."

Carrie giggled, and her posture relaxed. "It is?" Her eyes darted back to where she'd left me. When she didn't find me, she looked around for a second longer then gave Adam her attention.

"Yeah. That's probably weird, huh?" Adam scratched the side of his neck.

"Maybe to someone else," Carrie said, "but I get it. Its one of my favorites too."

"What can I get you?" A bartender asked her.

"Guinness."

"You're a dark beer girl?" Adam asked.

"That I am."

When the bartender set the beer in front of Carrie, Adam said, "Put it on mine."

She grinned at Adam who tapped her beer with his.

I floated down the crowded bar, only lowering myself to the floor when I was beside Rupert. I found his hand, and even though mine was invisible, he squeezed it back.

"Looks like we did it," he said, whispering right into my ear. Even without being able to see me, he knew exactly where it was.

After a few moments pressed close to Rupert, enjoying the feeling of being close to him, he ran a hand up my back and gave my waist a squeeze. I flew up and out of the way, as he made his way to Carrie and Adam.

"You Adam?" Rupert said, taking the space beside him.

"Rhett?" Rupert nodded. "Here you go." Rupert fished a phone out of his pocket and slid it to Adam on the bar top.

"Thanks, man," Adam said, shaking Rupert's hand. "I don't know how I lost it."

"Found it on the sidewalk."

Adam pushed his hand through his hair. "Thanks again," he said, turning back to Carrie.

Rupert walked into the bathroom and flew out a moment later.

"Ready?" I asked, flying above the crowd to meet him.

I'd begged Shanae, pleading with her to let this one Kiss slide, but she'd been firm, Rupert and I were already one couple left unKissed too many. There was no way she'd be able to explain Adam and Carrie to Charlotte. I knew she was right, but I'd been determined to make them meet naturally.

"Ready." I squeezed Rupert's hand and flew down to the boy I almost loved and Kissed him. When Carrie finished telling him about the door she was working on, I Kissed her too.

The sparks flew off their lips, and the cord shot between them. It took less than a second for the ends to find each other. Their bodies moved an inch closer, and their eyes locked. Carrie's neck flushed when Adam's eyes shifted to her lips. His Adam's apple bobbed just before he bit his bottom lip. She wrapped her fingers around the sleeve of his shirt, and he tucked a tendril of curls behind her ear. She was the one who went in for the kiss.

Their lips touched and the fireworks I'd been waiting for exploded off of them, Sealing their Kiss.

"How does it feel?" Rupert asked, grabbing both of my hands and pulling me higher into the air.

"It feels good."

"No regrets?"

"None." To prove it, I pulled Rupert into a kiss, showing him exactly how happy I was with the way everything turned out.

The band started up, playing a slow jazzy song. Rupert and I danced above the crowd, twirling and swaying to the music, wrapped in each other's arms like we'd always meant to be.

Chapter Thirty-Six

$\mathcal{T}$wo weeks later, my palms were sweating as Rupert and I flew into Cupid HQ hand in hand.

"You're sure about this?" I asked him.

"Absolutely." He stopped me before we went through the doors of the conference room. "And if they say no, we'll find a way to do it anyway."

"They can take our Kiss and Veils permanently for even suggesting it."

"They can have them," he said. "They can't take my lips, so I'll still be able to kiss you. And if they take our Veils, Lana will fly us to the city where we can live our lives like everyone else."

"They'd end our Hundred."

"So, I'll watch what I eat." He kissed the mole on the side of my face. "I'm in this with you, Freya."

My heart swelled, knowing I'd hit Destiny's jackpot. Even without a Kiss Sealing us together, Rupert and I were the real deal.

"I love you," I said.

"I love you. Let's do this."

Rupert and I stood in front of the same panel of Pavers that had suspended me. All except Daphne; she was permanently relocated.

Shanae gave me an encouraging nod, and I dropped Rupert's hand, stepping forward, ready to put my cards on the table.

Rupert had wanted to be the one to talk, to receive the full backlash if it came to that, but I insisted. This was my idea. My plan. I wouldn't let Rupert take the first hit.

I wouldn't be able to protect him from being guilty by association though. He was in this with me.

"I hope you've learned something from all of this," Bill said, peering over his glasses.

"I've learned a lot, sir. A whole lot."

Charlotte let out an exhausted sigh. "Good. I'm glad this is finally behind us. It's been hard making up for the two of you these last couple of weeks. It was made especially difficult to be down one Cupid, let alone two." She glared at Rupert. "I hope your vacation was worth all of the catchup you'll have to do."

"Worth every second," Rupert said, and I didn't have to turn to look at him to know he was using his dirty smile.

Charlotte rolled her eyes, confirming my suspicion. "You will remain on probation for another month, Freya. Shanae will be auditing you closely to make sure you stay on track."

"About that," I said, swallowing hard. "I can't go back to work."

Bill took off his glasses and laid them on the stack of papers on the table.

"Not like before, anyways." I let out a shaky breath before continuing. "I believe in what we do. I do. But I don't believe in how we do it."

"Neither do I." Rupert's arm touched the small of my back as he came to stand beside me.

"I've been Kissed."

"We know." Charlotte glared at Rupert. "Everyone knows."

I blushed. "I don't mean like that. I mean I've received Cupid's Kiss."

"That we know, too."

"It's not right. Not natural. We exist to make sure Destiny comes to be, but people are still meant to have free will. If I hadn't recognized what was happening to me, I would be living my life with the wrong man."

"That's ridiculous," Charlotte said. "We would have broken it. There is no way we would have let you throw away your Destiny like that."

"That might be the case," I said, feeling even more nervous.

"But that doesn't make it any less true that my free will had been compromised."

"It was a mistake. It should have never happened," Bill said. "The responsible party will pay for that mistake for the rest of her life."

I wasn't getting anywhere the way I was going about it, so I just came out and said it. "I want the policy to change. I want Cupid's to be assigned to their couples a month in advance. I want them to help them find each other organically. And only after they've committed to each other—willingly—do we enact the Kiss to strengthen their bond."

Shanae gave me a smile but wiped it off when Charlotte tracked my gaze.

"Impossible," Bill said. "You have no idea how much manpower that would require."

"I do, actually. I did it two weeks ago in one night."

"That was one time," Bill said.

"I do it all of the time. Not every couple, no, but a lot of them, and that's when I was working with a one-week deadline. Once a two people form a natural bond, the Kiss Seals itself, usually in a matter of minutes."

"Why are we still listening to this?" Bill asked.

"Because she's right," Charlotte said.

Rupert squeezed my hand.

"When I was in the field—centuries ago—Cupid's were given a year. And they had to be granted permission to use their Kiss."

"This isn't the Middle Ages," Bill said. "The population is out of control. People move about the country and overseas on a whim. There are too many of them and not enough of us. We've had to evolve with the times. No one knows that more than you, Charlotte."

"And no one knows how much we've sacrificed while evolving more than I do."

"Did you know about this?" Bill asked Shanae.

She looked at her shoes.

"What you're asking," Charlotte said, "can't be accomplished overnight. Nor can I promise it can be accomplished at all. We are just one of thousands of Clouds filled with millions of

Pavers."

"We know," Rupert said.

"But, everything has to start somewhere." Charlotte smiled. "This is your plan"—she pointed to Rupert and me—"You have to figure out how it will work. We'll give you access to your assignments a month in advance. If and when you have proven a system that works, we'll implement it throughout our Cupids."

"You're not serious," Bill said.

"I'm very serious. I don't claim to know what Destiny has planned, but I'd be willing to bet my Wings that these two are meant to do this."

Bill grunted.

"But Freya, Rupert," Charlotte said. "I will put an end to this if you miss even one deadline."

Chapter Thirty-Seven

Six months later, Rupert and I shared a bag of popcorn while sitting on the lowest limb of an oak tree in our last trial assignment's front yard.

DeMarcus Williams and Emma Chen had been the toughest of our assignments to match up organically. They lived on opposite sides of the metroplex, were ten years apart in age, and didn't have a single apparent thing in common. But as the weeks went by, and Rupert and I feared we weren't going to pull it off, we picked away at their surfaces until we found a shared passion for outer space. Neither of them harbored secret desires to become astronauts or were trying to make their passion into their professions, but time and again, we witnessed them pausing their night to walk outside and look up at the stars.

Rupert and I took on the task of orchestrating a star-gazing event. We'd picked a night neither of them had anything going on and plastered flyers everywhere we thought they might see them.

We'd loaded a small yacht with every Paver in our inner circle and waited for them to show up. Rupert spent the whole day memorizing facts and learning the sky, but once Emma introduced herself to DeMarcus, they didn't even care about hearing the promised lesson. They found a secluded spot on the end of the boat, and they spent the evening finding constellations on their own.

They'd kissed several times over their follow-up date tonight, but it wasn't until their date was over that I'd performed Cupid's Kiss. The next time their lips touched, their job would be officially done.

"Here it is." Rupert kissed the top of my head, wrapping his arm around me. "The big Kiss."

Emma said something to DeMarcus, and he went in for what looked like would be a goodnight kiss, but as the fireworks exploded off their lips, the kiss deepened and went on for much longer than I was comfortable watching. Eventually, Emma pulled away long enough to unlock her door, and DeMarcus followed her in.

"I think that's our cue to leave." I patted Rupert's knee and readied myself for takeoff.

"Not so fast." He caught my waist before I could fly away.

"Oh, come one," I said, "even you know better than to watch through the windows."

He laughed, shooting me a smile that made me question whether or not he did know better.

"Rupert!"

"Give me some credit and wait a minute."

I waited, wondering what I was waiting for. He did something on his phone, shielding me from seeing what it was exactly.

"Why are you acting sneaky?"

But he was looking at the lawn in front of us instead of looking at me. I stared at it, waiting for something to happen. When the wind blew the blades of grass around, I shivered.

"It's supposed to freeze tonight. Can we do whatever it is we're doing somewhere warmer."

He ignored me and looked at his phone again, this time worry lines creased his face.

"What's going on?"

He kept staring at the grass, so I did too.

Then, blinking out of nowhere, sat a tiny grey dog with floppy ears and a curly tail.

Stunned, and only wondering where it came from for long enough to realize it didn't matter, the poor thing must be freezing, I launched off the tree branch and went straight for the dog, pulling it into my arms and shielding it from the cold as much as I could.

"Where did you come from?" I nuzzled my face into its

neck, loving the feel of its soft fur on my skin. "Someone must be so worried about you." I searched for a collar, hoping its owner had given him a tag. The collar was pink and studded with tiny gemstones. "Where are your parents, girly?" There was no tag with an address or phone number. Where it should have been, was a diamond ring.

I turned to Rupert, wondering if he was seeing what I was seeing.

Rupert wasn't in the tree where I'd left him.

He was in the grass, bent on one knee.

I opened my mouth to wonder why he was there, but before I asked, I knew.

"Freya,"

"Yes!" I said, hugging the dog closer to me and flying toward him.

"I haven't asked you anything."

"Yes," I said again.

"You're kind of ruining this for me."

"Right." I sniffled and wiped away tears that were threatening to freeze on my face. "Go ahead."

"Freya, will you make my dreams come true and marry me?"

I nodded, suddenly unable to speak. The lump in my throat was too big.

"You will?"

"Yes, of course, yes."

He got to his feet and pulled the dog from my arms so he could free the ring from her collar.

I was kissing him as he slipped the ring onto my finger. The little dog licked our chins.

Clapping came from all around us, and I pulled away from the little cocoon the three of us were in to discover the source of the sound.

Lana's hands were clasped at her chest, her eyes glistening with happy tears. Penny was jumping up and down, clapping like an excited little girl. Percy looked at Penny like she'd lost her mind, but when his eyes fell on mine, he smiled.

Shanae was there too, so were Charlotte and Mariah.

Marisol walked up to me, kissing me on the cheek. Before

she pulled away, she said, "You've done it, honey. This is your Destiny, and you've chosen it for yourself."

I looked at him. To Rupert. And knew she was right. All this time waiting, he was my Destiny and everything we'd do together.

The End

CPSIA information can be obtained
at www.ICGtesting.com
Printed in the USA
FSHW021934190320
68150FS